MASTERS OF THE MAZE

Wildside Press Books
by Avram Davidson

Clash of Star-Kings
The Enemy of My Enemy
Island Under the Earth
Joyleg (with Ward Moore)
The Kar-Chee Reign / Rogue Dragon
Marco Polo and the Sleeping Beauty (with Grania
Masters of the Maze
Peregrine: Primus
Peregrine: Secundus
Rork!
Ursus of Ultima Thule

MASTERS OF THE MAZE

by Avram Davidson

WILDSIDE PRESS
BERKELEY HEIGHTS • NEW JERSEY

MASTERS OF THE MAZE

For Poul and Karen Anderson, Marion Zimmer Bradley,
Walter Breen, Ted Cogswell, Grania Davidson, Phil Dick,
Ray and Kirsten Nelson.

First Wildside Press edition: April 2000.

Unless the past perishes, I cannot be safe.
—PETRARCH

Elias Ashmole thought that he had discovered it. Oxford lawyer, courtier, soldier, astrologer, alchemist, historian, mystic, pragmatist, devotee of the new learning as well as the old; first gentleman freemason, founder of the first "public museum of curiosities" in England: Elias Ashmole, *floreat* 1617-1692.

The Maze was, is, and will be. When the magnablock exploded into infinity, the Maze was formed. "There was light"—and the light shone upon the Maze. Coeval and coexistent, neither of the same substance nor the same essence; having the attributes, the incidents, the accidents of neither terrene nor contraterrene matter, the Maze is both immanent and transcendent of both. It traverses space, it transects time. Ancient of years, the worlds form around it. . . .

The nearest and quickest way is not ever the best. There is a door by which one can enter the treasure house of Croesus—but although it is only a hundred steps from door to treasure, fifty of these steps pass through the house of Daniel Dickensheet in Mincemeat Lane in the year of the Plague and on the door of that house is painted a cross, and the words, *Lord Have Mercy On Us.* . . .

Generation after generation, generation before generation, north and south and up and down, the early and the latter rains, and the great red slow-rolling sun of the End of Days, have seen, see, and have yet to see the Masters of the Maze at their work. They explore, they plot their courses, they watch. Perhaps this above all. They watch. They guard.

CHAPTER ONE

Darius Chauncey had been in his time attached to the staff of General Logan, and thus (besides other good and sufficient reasons) should have been aware of the importance of keeping a vigilant picket. But Darius Chauncey was also the lover of the local Snake Goddess, and the thought of her firm and painted breasts and her hips, so supple beneath the flouncy skirts, had beguiled him. And so the Chulpex got by, silent, swift, and pale as wax. He was at any event observed by Et-dir-Mor, a High Physicist of the Red Fish People, and Et-dir-Mor sped to cut him off. But the way was exceptionally intricate and by the time it was half-traversed the Chulpex had vanished. He was, as it happened, soon enough apprehended elsewhere on an outside. His captors showed him a cross and he hissed knowingly and bowed before it—unwisely, as he soon learned, for they at once dealt with him in the name of Perunas (to whom they were still faithful), hooting in astonishment at the curious things the fire was doing to his body. And he was soon dead.

Et-dir-Mor had had some notion that this might be the case, but he returned in a rather thoughtful mood nonetheless. It did seem to him that more Chulpex than usual were being sighted. He made a note to discuss it with Ambrose Bierce.

Joseph Bellamy sat at his heaped-up desk trying to catch up with correspondence dealing with the Esquires of the Sword. From time to time he glanced automatically at an object on the far left corner of the desk-top, a truncated pyramid of something resembling a faintly roseate crystal with a curiously fractured pattern of lines inside of it. Now and then he looked appreciatively at the fire of great greasy black slabs of bituminous burning in his fireplace grate: eighty percent of the heat of course went right up the vast fieldstone chimney, but Joseph Bellamy did not care. Though

9

he was bundled up snugly, he considered too much warmth to be unhealthy, conducive to colds.

Right Worthy and Worshipful Compeer: (he wrote) *Pray accept my arms and my esteem in the name of Elias and the Vigil.* He paused in his muttering, and the sturdy though ancient typewriter with its bank of keys on either side fell silent.

Been trying to get hold of you by phone, he went on, after a moment, *but the service up here in this part of the state is enough to give indigestion to a sow. And they have the nerve to want an increase in rates, too! Ess aitch dash tee, is what I say to that, and now to business, if not labor. I have been well aware of the Eleventh Sequence recently and I know that a good reason exists for things having been slack. But you know that I am fairly isolated up here where I am and at the moment it is simply impossible to replace you. I will ask around and see what can be done. There is someone on whom I have my eye. So try and take care of your health for the time being. I—*

He glanced again at the dawn-colored and translucent ward on the corner of his desk, frowned, clicked his tongue; typed, at a quickened pace, *I conclude without conclusion and remain, Right Worthy and Worshipful Compeer, yours in Elias and the Vigil which is never concluded,* Jos ∴ Bellamy ESQ ∴ ESLU †

He picked up something long and withy-thin with a short crosspiece near the lower end. He proceeded. He said to the one he presently faced, "Go back. For you there is never passage. Back. Go. Go now."

Pallid, thin, faintly glistening, something which might have been "Gold" or "Cold" sounded. Arms were waved. Hiss and hiss and breathy syllables.

"Go back. Back. Go."

The thing in Bellamy's hand glowed with a faintly blue-green light in the obscurity. He thrust. He moved.

"Old. Old. Much cold. Much gold. Nay. Stay. Ss. P . . ."

Wearily, wearily, Joseph Bellamy proceeded. Sound died away to a thin thread which was merely awareness. The figure receded, turned, receded, twisted, turned, dwindled, turned upside down, wiggled, shrank, reversed, vanished.

Bellamy sighed, shivered, withdrew.

The blaze was welcome for its sight and sound as well as warmth, and he thought (as very often) of Adam Cadmon, Adam Androgyne, the Primal Mother-Father, facing fire for the first incredible time: the beckoning-repelling comfort-fear of the ever-beautiful flux of it. The constant-inconstant dancing heart of it. Eternal promise, eternal dream.

He sighed, he sighed and returned to his desk.

Nathaniel Gordon stared at his face in the mirror. Hopeless—quite hopeless! Brow too low, nose too blunt, teeth too large, ears— For the thousandth time he thought of covering all (or a goodly part of the all) with a beard. But the thought of two to three weeks of itch and ugliness dissuaded him. Although now and here was the logical time and place if it were ever to be done.

He thought once again, lovingly, longingly, of the long-planned trip to Europe. Three-quarters of the way around the Mediterranean (. . ."*tideless, dolorous midland sea . . . land of sand and ruin and gold . . .*"), then leave the ship at Trieste and— And here, as always, the torture of indecision.

Which way? To the east, the picturesque and unpeopled . . . comparatively . . . by tourists . . . the Balkans? Oots and sooks and slivova. Pre-Sarajevoan inns in hidden valleys. Dollars stretching endlessly. Glagolitic alphabets, glades buried in attarous roses plucked by half-naked and lascivious xenophile peasant girls. Black lambs and gray falcons. And also: political police, mass calisthenics, fleas, fierce scowling knife-bearing xenophobic peasant *men*. Or to the west, the familiar, the necessary, the source and fount, the tamed and undangerous, the tourist-swarming, expensive, dollarophagic, accessible . . .

He grunted, abandoned the mirror, returned to the typewriter. East or west, whichever was best, Nate Gordon would never make either one (Sardinian town perched on crag, Frisian fishing village, Paris the beautiful and ever-receptive, wild Wales) (Illyrian Jonina of the false messiah, thyme-and-lilac scented Chios, Diocletian-haunted Dalmatia) if he did not raise the essential fund.

And it was well within his grasp, he *could* do it. All he had to do was sit down at the mill and grind out ten pieces at $400 each. Or twenty at $200 each. Or some combination or permutation thereof. He had editorial okays. He knew the style and craft, the market. Love-Starved Arabs Raped Me Often. Communist Crocodiles Raped My Wife. Man-Eaters of the Malayan Peninsula. Man-Hating Women Pirates of Polynesia. Women-Eating Arabs of the Crocodile Coast. Get the guy up on the cliff. Leave him up there. Explain how he got there. Then get him off of there. Down off, up off, it made no difference. Rabid Bats Devoured My Wife. Woman-Eating Crocodiles of Wild Bokhara. Rasputin Raped My Aunt.

He had written such pieces a hundred times before, each under a different name (only sometimes he forgot and used some of them over again, so that poor Pierce Tarraval, to name but one, had lost wives to fates worse than death on three different continents), each provided with a pseudonymous affidavit attesting to its authenticity—and each had sold promptly.

"Really," simpered his slightly fey agent, who knew the manly men's magazine market like the inside of his posh apartment; "Really, Nathaniel, such versatile Fertility!"

"Stick with me, kid, and I'll wrap your ass in silk."

The money had come in easily, and, just as easily, it had gone right out again. It had all been easy and effortless then. And then Nate discovered that he no longer wanted to write such easy, profitable crap. He wanted to write things harder, better, with his own name on them, things that would be a pride and a comfort to you, which the others were not, even if the money was spent just as fast—things you could keep on a shelf and take down and open from time to time and look at and show to others—that you could just *think* about from time to time and be glad about.

Nothing that he had written so far was like that. Not that he regretted what he had written so far. He had, so to speak, starved in his last garret and slept on his (or, rather, some-one else's) last living room sofa: that scene, so romantic to some, held no more allure for him. He had a comfortable apartment in the Seventies, and he was glad to have it. He was glad to be able to eat good meals of his own providing and not to have to walk twenty blocks in the cold in hopes of being invited to stay to a much less good meal at someone else's not-so-comfortable apartment. He was able to drink good booze when he felt like it—and he felt like it only as often as he felt like it—and not, when desperation descended, to have to roam from one saloon to another looking for a lonely and babbling lush who might after an incalculable wait invite him to have a shot of bar whiskey.

His improved circumstances and improved self-confidence enabled him to satisfy other needs and hungers, too. It had seemed to Nate, when he had no place to take a girl, that the only girls he could find were those who had no place to take a fellow. It was said that the English made love (if you could call it that) in alleys, standing up. You could hardly do that in New York. Now, at any rate, he didn't even need to think about it, having his choice of two beds and a sofa (as well as a few thick rugs) on which to make love to girls with large breasts and girls with small breasts and girls with hardly any breasts at all (not that the lack of them mattered if you kept your mind on fundamentals), to girls who smelled sweetly and girls who smelled naturally (sometimes almost *too* naturally), and girls who had no smell at all, to girls who were push-button ready and girls who took forever to get ready and girls . . .

No. Nate no longer desired to think in terms of girls, plural. The question now was of *a* girl. *The* girl. That is, when the question wasn't one of writing. Whatever it might have been if things had developed somewhat differently, the two questions were now really one question.

"*You*," she had said, "are prostituting yourself."

The more he felt the force of the charge, the more he denied its accuracy, the more she held to it. Her name was Peggy Stone, she was perfectly ordinary looking, she was warm and kind and loving and (after more patience and persuasion than he was accustomed to) good in bed. So Nate had asked himself why he should look further. Then he asked Peggy. And she told him.

"I make a good living," he protested.

"So do I. Already."

"But you wouldn't have to work—"

"I enjoy working."

"But what if we have kids?"

" '*We?*' "

He stared at her, his face askew and aggrieved. "You mean you don't want to marry me?"

"Very much. But."

And the *But* brought them right back where they'd started from. She wouldn't marry him as long as, capable of writing better, he continued to write rubbish. No, she didn't want him (as he suggested, sarcastically) to contribute "experimental writing" to little magazines that paid in free copies . . . when they paid at all.

"If you were just Johnny-One-Note, that would be something else," she said. "I still wouldn't like the crud you churn out on your little crud-mill"—here she gestured to his antediluvian portable. "—but I'd . . . I wouldn't *grin* and bear it,

I'd just bear it. But you *aren't* Johnny One-Note. Those things you wrote for *America West*—"

Here he stopped being sullen and sorry, leaped into sound and struggle. What did she mean, *things*? He had written, for *America West* exactly one—"One, count them, one!"—article. And had been paid a total of $17 for it! Peggy was unconvinced. And the Hell of it was, so was Nate Gordon.

He knew he could do better, he wanted to do better, had been long on the verge of coming to the same conclusion—and was still in this regard, he grumblingly told himself, *virgo intacto*. Perhaps matters, if left to themselves, might have worked out so as to allow him to make his own change in his own way. As it was— Well, as it was, it wasn't going to be easy. For one thing, he had to make a complete break away from the familiar scene. For one thing, could he—there in the old apartment—write anything but the old sludge? It was doubtful. Too, if he went on living in the same place there would be the constant demands of the old life. Liquor store, restaurants, friends, bars, bookstores, theaters, girls, girls, girls—all costing money at the same old rate. He would *have* to go on churning out the same old crud.

Also—Jamieson Swift, his agent—and Lew Sharp, Burt Nash, Sydney Sherman, editors of the magazines Nate contemptuously named to himself as *Brute, Rut,* and *Gonad*—would they leave him alone to work out his destiny in the fashion he would have to grope for? No, no they would not. And could he resist them, if they came pleading and cajoling and doling out fat, tempting advances? No, no he could not.

Therefore, there was only one solution: Get away. And, he told himself, if he had to get away, it made sense to get away as far away as possible. Where, for one thing, nobody would be bothering him not to change; where, for another, the demands of money would be absent; and where, perhaps most essential of all, where he could let the winds of far-off places blow through his mind and clear it of accustomed clichés and contrivances, formulas and familiar fancies.

The answer (he told himself, as authors old and young and now dead and still living have told themselves so often)— the answer was Europe.

It was only by chance that the way to Europe seemed to lie by way of Darkglen Woods, the estate of Joseph Bellamy.

Flint's Forge has long been cold, and the living cannot

remember when it was ever hot. The village to which it gave
its name has withered away to something less than a hamlet,
and no one but an occasional hunter or berry picker ever
lights on the buckling stone walls of the old ironworkers'
houses off in the woods, or smells the scent of their lilac
bushes, now grown into trees.

The narrow road hereabouts is bordered for the most part
with thicket and woods, crowding in close enough (except at
high noon) to shut off much light: pine and sumac and
Chinese elm. In scattered places some pasture is still kept
open enough to give a view of farther woods in ever-darken-
ing shades of green rising up into the hills and the low
mountains. Here and there an old small house clings to the
lip of the road, timbers sagging and never painted and now
blackening with very age; and sometimes an old man or old
woman, fat and toothless, sits in a chair on the warping
porch, waves to the infrequent passing aquaintance, stares—
less in suspicion than astonishment—at the rare passing stranger.

At one point the road rises high and sheers close to a drop
where the land falls away abruptly and far, and shows, off in
the middle distance, the river bending like a bow. Here, on
the other side of the road, are set two one-story houses and
one two-story house, and the ground floor of the latter is
occupied by a small general store which sells beer and gaso-
line as well.

Quite early one afternoon in the late spring of the year the
sound of an automobile was heard by three men lounging
around in the store.

"Who's *that*, I wonder?" asked a stumpy-looking man with
a seamed face.

"You ought to know, George, it's your store." Amused by
his wit, the speaker, a fattish older fellow dressed in greasy
lumber-jacket, overalls, and a dirty union suit, spread his
almost toothless mouth in hissing laughter.

George ignored him. "Coming up from town, it sounds
like," he said, addressing the third person there. "Wonder . . . Hey, Jack?" Jack was about thirty, with a dark,
brooding face. He made no answer. After a moment he got
up and moved to the door. George followed him, and, when
the noise of the motor had grown louder, so did the heavy
old man. Something came into sight and showed where the
road curved across a fold in the hill.

"Yep . . . coming up from town," said George.

Prefacing his remarks with a few heavy breaths, the old-ster said, "Nicky Flint drove down this morning. Didn' he, Jack? But that ain't never his car. Hey Jack?" The dark young man said nothing. The older man scratched his armpit comfortably. "Nicky Flint drove down this morning, I says. Didn' he, Jack?"

"Where Major Flint goes is none of your business."

The old man laughed again, hissing and showing his tooth-less gums like a fat old lizard. Then the car itself passed by, long and sleek and luminous. "Jesus Montgomery Christ!" exclaimed George, deeply impressed. "Would you look at that thing!"

Jack's face was bright. The old man pursed his lips and scratched the dirty white stubble on his jowls. "Lookst a me like a one a them, oh, now, I saw one years ago in the city, hey now, yeah. A Roolds-Royst."

Before he had altogether finished, Jack said, quickly, "It's a Bentley."

"I'd 'a' said you was right, Jeff—"

"No, it's a Bentley, George—"

"Lookst a me," Jeff repeated, stubbornly wagging his head, "like a Roolds-Royst."

"It's more or less the same make of car, only—" The automobile vanished from their sight. The curtain descended on Jack's face, the brooding look returned.

"Wonder who that could *be*," the proprietor said. "Was that your boss in the car, could you see, Jack? I think there was a good four people there."

The dark man said nothing, but old Jeff had a point or two of comment. "Say, you know all about them makes of cars, don't you, Jack. I didn' think you was interested. I thought all you was interested in was women and jack-light-ing deer." He paused. "Hey Jack?" He picked at his nose. "Speaking of which, how is your new woman? Your new-est one, I sh'd say."

Jack shrugged. "Good enough. They all got the same thing."

"Yeh-es," Jeff nodded, judiciously. "But some of 'm's got more of it than others . . . If I had me a new woman, young one, say, I shouldn' like to be leaving her alone all night whiles I was setting at the bottom of a mineshaft . . . un-less she was setting there with me. . . ."

Jack threw him a look in which a thin flash of his teeth showed. Instantly Jeff seemed to become much older, sillier, devoid of possibility of harmful intention. He breathed steamily, waddled back to his chair.

George, still thoughtful, said, "Suppose, maybe, some *land* syndicate could be interested in maybe putting up a big hotel or a lot of cottages . . . or something . . . no . . ." He shook his head.

Jeff smacked his knee loudly. "Hey now, I know what it is! Why sure. 'Mineshaft,' that's what put it into my head. Bet you a penny to a pot of peas that Nicky Flint is trying to interest another sucker in that old piss-worthless mine of his! Hey?"

George slowly cut himself a slice of headcheese and nibbled on it. "Mmm . . . That could be, I suppose. He's had investors out there before, I believe. But . . . worthless? If it was worthless, how come they've held onto it, all these years?"

The old man slid forward about an inch. "How come is right. Keep the fences mended and all. And keep guards on duty twenty-four hours a day. Tell what it is you're guarding down there, hey Jack? Gold? Dye-muns? You-ranium?"

His mind seemingly mostly on other things, Jack mumbled, "Guarding the pit-props, keep some dirty old jackass like you from stealing them for firewood."

Jeff hissed and quivered. Next, more soberly, he said, "I wonder when the last carload of ore was took up out of that mine. *I* don't remember it. My father didn't remember it, neither. Old Tom Shoot, he claimed he did, but he was such an awful old liar, used to claim he was in the Rebellion and all such lies as that."

George finished the slice of headcheese and sucked on his teeth. "They weren't always pure lies, you know, Jeff. His mind got kind of weak a long ways before he died. He used to get mixed up between what he seen and what he'd heard told of others seeing. I know he claimed there was goblins down there and that's why they quit mining. But he also claimed he recalled when the green timber was cut to make boats to fight the British, and I know that did happen, heard other old people tell of having heard of it."

After a moment he added, almost reluctantly, "Tom Shoot's great-grandmother, she was that famous white-witch-woman, so they said."

Jeff, not smiling, said in a lower voice, "Nettie Wishert. Yes . . ."

In the silence following, Jack said, as though to himself

and as though from a long ways off, "But I'll have one yet. You wait and see."

Instantly alert and keen, Jeff asked, "A Bintley?"

The dark young man's guard was down and for a moment his expression was slack and astonished. Surprise and anger struggled in his face. Then it tightened and his eyes closed part-way down.

"I don't get just my wages and free house and truck garden," he said. "I get free cartridges, too. All I want."

Jeff's mouth pursed his absolute innocence, utter incomprehension. "Take a pile of cartridges to buy one a them Bintleys," he piped. "Still . . . if Major Nick Flint told you you'd get one, why, hmmm, ymmm . . . He's a great one for promises. It runs in the family. I believe the old general promised Nettie Wishert something, too. Or was it the other way round? Hey George?"

But George only wondered aloud whose car that might have been. And Jack's eyes blazed in his dark and brooding face.

The hands of John Joseph Horn were large and immaculately groomed and thatched with colorless hair through which showed the pigmented areas which used to be called "liver spots." The hands moved now on the velvety wool of the carriage rug covering his lap and legs, picked up a brochure, glanced into it.

. . . *particularly the property known as The Old General Mine, which has been in the hands of the Flint family since granted by George II . . .*

. . . *reason to believe that the application of modern scientific methods to the refining and extractive processes would repay investment many times over and . . .*

Horn grunted very slightly, gently but firmly laid the brochure aside, picked up a little booklet bound in leather, opened it with one finger in a gesture which somehow managed to be almost priestly, took out the blue silk ribbon marker, ran his finger down the page (foxed as the back of his hand), found the place he sought.

. . . *maintaining that part of the Great Mysterie or Secret Tradition given through the Teutonic Knights, who brought the Teaching and Discipline of the Great White Christ to the last European pagans . . .*

Horn thrust out his lower lip—"M-*hm*, m-*hm*"—then looked up and over at the man sitting at the opposite window, a man of approximately his own age, with a long, dark face, grizzled hair cut close to the long skull. "Major," said Horn, "my stomach tells me it's one o'clock. Would you be kind enough to reach down into that case and pour me a cup of what's in that thermos bottle? I thank you. I thank you."

He sipped, made a grateful noise in his nose. "This cup contains *milk*," he said; "pure *milk*, with none of its essential bacteria destroyed by the murderous method of pasteurization, and made hot over a gentle flame but not boiled. It comes from one of my own dairy herds, a crossbreed of Jersey and Red Hindi which has been developed under my own supervision over a course of thirty years, and fed on purely organic fodder grown on purely organically fertilized fields. It contains a specific quantity of mildly toasted natural wheat heart produced by the same process, and a small amount of raw sugar from which none of the essentials have been extracted by so-called refining. It is, I do not hesitate to say, *the* most *healthful* food-drink available to modern man. There is another cup in the case, if you would care to try it."

Major Flint turned his head and gazed at Horn squarely with his yellow-brown eyes. "I never drink milk," he said.

"Drink whiskey, I suppose."

"No. I can't afford whiskey."

Horn sucked back his lower lip with a little smacking sound. "I like the way you said that. No whining. No disgrace to being honestly poor, why can't people *realize* that? instead of yelping and sniffling and begging for hand-outs? Particularly none in being lead-poor." He drank the rest of his milk, absently held out the empty cup. After a second Major Flint took it and put it back in the case.

"Well. KLEL." He tapped the cover of the little book as he repeated the word embossed there. "I don't mind telling you, I was a bit dubious at first. Never heard of it, said to myself. Sounds clandestine, said to myself. But. When you told me the names of some of the other members—Governor Shank. Henry O'Dowd. Baron Fish—I checked."

Flint looked over his shoulder at the passing countryside. Turning back, he said, stiffly, "KLEL was registered with the Grand Consistory of Rites in Paris in 1788. Naturally, during the tragic events which followed, it dropped from sight. Experience may be a bitter teacher, but She is a good one. Once the benefits of working in silence were realized, they were never forgotten. KLEL is not now and it never has been—*clandestine.* It is now, it always has been, and it will always continue to be—*selective.*"

John Joseph Horn nodded. "I know," he said. "I checked," he repeated. "Harry O'Dowd told me all about you. Your family's impeccable record. Your own service—in war and peace. Your struggles to hold on to your property, your struggles to hold your own in business despite being up to your neck surrounded by Jews and Irish and Italians; well, we all know what New York is like. Your staunch support of the various constitutionalist causes, despite all evidence that you could often ill afford it. I checked, Major, I checked it all, up and down, Harry O'Dowd or no Harry O'Dowd. I might say that I was not least impressed by the fact that you never allowed any of our fellow patriots to throw business your way, refused to sharpen your personal axe on the grindstone, so to speak."

The car sped down a low hill, toiled up a high one, rounded one curve after another. "Nothing noble about that," growled Major Flint. "I am beholden to no one, and I intend to keep it that way. I didn't take advantage of my privilege as the GC of KLEL to make you a member on sight just because you're rich. There's a man named Jack Pace, his father was one of my grandfather's bastards, but that's neither here nor there; Jack Pace is at the mine for $35 a week, and I made *him* one on sight.

"Rich men? My *God!*" he cried, "the *B'nai Brith* is rotten with rich men! The *Mafia* is rotten with rich men! And those damned Englishmen up there in Canada are so rotten-rich from the lumber and the ore they sell us and the wheat they sell Red China, that—that—" His nostrils flared, he clenched his teeth.

"Why," he said in a lower, calmer, yet even more scornful voice, "*there are rich niggers!*"

John Joseph Horn nodded slowly, sadly.

No, no, Major Flint wanted it made clear, it was not just Horn's money alone which mattered in this thing. It was the fact that he had the right idea about the use of money. "The whole world kicks us around as they please. Communists, Catholics, taking over all around! When is it going to end? And where? We've got the key—KLEL. We've even got a keyhole—" He gestured up ahead of him. Then his mouth twisted and he sat back in the seat.

"But it doesn't fit," he murmured. "It doesn't fit."

Some hours later the two of them sat in the bare, musty old shack which served as the "office" of the Delaware and National Mining Company. "Well, now you've seen it and now you know," said Major Flint. "You're one of the Elect, you've been a Knight, you're now a Commander. According to our *Doctrines and Degrees,* any Grand Commander can—with any two other Commanders—pass himself and themselves and any others of the second degree onto the third: Lord Commander. But General Flint, the first GC, laid it down that this was not to be done until a better Gate was found. And we've been playing it so quietly ever since, lying so low, that we haven't . . . we don't . . . Well . . ."

Horn picked up the three pieces of gold upon the table, shook them in his hand, put them down again. "A better Gate. *Twelve gates into the City.* I suppose there must be even more than twelve."

Flint shrugged. More than twelve million, he supposed. A bitter smile touched his long, dark face briefly. "But it seems to be a case of, You can't get there from here. God knows we've tried, we've been trying for a hundred and seventy years, at least."

"And it hasn't changed? No, eh? I'm shaken, Flint. As you may suppose. No one ever saw anything like that—what you showed me. It can't be described, it couldn't even be dreamed of. *But it exists!* Yet . . . you say, You can't get there from here." He shoved the gold pieces with his fingers and they clinked. "*Some*one must've gotten there from here. And brought back . . . just these? Who was it?"

It was an old woman named Nettie Wishert. Yes, she'd been initiated. Yes, that was probably irregular. But there were other occasions in the eighteenth century, Lady Aldsworth, for example. Anyway, Wishert had had her own Mysterie, in a way, and she was brave. She went through the Gate, and further on, and through an outside, and through another gate, and there she found the treasure house and she came back dragging a sack of gold coins. And these were all that still remained. Just three.

Horn picked them up and looked again. His face shone with awe. On one side were the foreparts of a bull and a lion facing each other. On the other, in a square divided into four squares were, in archaic Greek characters, the letters KPOIΣ BAΣIΛ.

"*Krois basil,*" said Flint. "Short for *Kroisou basileos.* King Croesus. Think, think!"

"Croesus, the man who invented money . . . Lord, man,

this may be the first money ever minted!" Horn's eyes gleamed. He wet his lips. "And why hasn't anyone ever gone back? Has it been closed? The Gate? Didn't your old woman ever want to go back? Or your ancestor? It seems to me that the key fit the keyhole well enough. So—"

Said Flint, "It's the outside that the Gate leads to, the place you've got to pass through before you can get anywhere else. We've checked and rechecked. There's no mistake. 'There was sickness in that house,' old Wishert said. 'Fever, and the evil fever, too.' "

Horn said, "Oh," flatly.

"She died in agony, cursing the General. And he died in agony, cursing her. And the gold lay where they'd spilled it for a good twenty years before any of my family would touch it. The nature of the disease was unmistakable. They died of plague."

This time Horn's "Oh" was faint and sickly. He started to push away the coins, stopped, shuddered, smiled—after a moment.

"Well. So we need another Gate. And that's where I come in, isn't it? Me . . . and my money. Where do we begin? I suppose you must have an idea, or you wouldn't have brought me here."

Flint nodded, curtly. He leaned the leather-patched elbows of his jacket on the worn old table. "There's a man named Bellamy," he said.

CHAPTER TWO

It was the characteristic breath-aura as it smoked its distinctive tints and colors in the chilly air which identified Arrettagorretta to the Na 14 'Parranto 600, although the 'Gorretta-Sire's vast size would have been identification enough.

The room was large and quite bare of graffitti; the Sire had no need of such low-nest indications of identity-assertion; and no one else, of course, would dare. So the Na bowed low, and let his breath out. For a while it seemed almost as though the Sire did not see him, so preoccupied he was. Then he said, "Take food, the Na."

"For strength to serve you." The Na politely placed his hands behind his back and bent over the indicated plate.

"Not so, not so. I wish to see you eat as do the vivipars. Have you not been trained, the Na? It was that I thought you had been trained." Arrettagorretta, the 'Gorretta-Sire, seemed not angry, but mildly surprised.

Hastily, "The Na had not been properly informed by those directed. Else he had suredly brought with him the necessary implements. Intelligent, chulpechoid vivipars generally take food with implements; this was impressed upon the Na during training."

The great Sire moved his massy head. "That is so, I had forgotten. There is so much to remember, and meanwhile, Sun Sarnis grows old, grows cold . . ."

The Na keened. It was the sensible thing to do. And stopped short when he saw the Sire about to speak again.

" 'Generally,' this means, the Na, not invariably. Hence it follows that vivipars, even intelligent chulpechoids, sometimes take food without implements. Therefore, the Na—" He watched as the Na took his hands from behind his back, searched the plate for a solid, took it in his hands and severed it, and so ate it. "I see. They eat as do the Sires. Interesting. But not surprising, seeing that among them each one is itself a Sire, or so I have heard. Enough, the Na."

Placing the remains of the solid near the plate, the Na waited and listened. He hoped that Arrettagorretta would spare him the inevitable drear-talk. "Let me see . . . You have been under training, so. Current Project Four. To occupy the designation Jacques or Jacksa. Or was it, the Na, Jackson?"

Showing no outward sign of inward feeling, the Na made a simple declaration that he had been under training, Current Project Five, occupying the designation Ten-pid-Ar.

Arrettagorretta seemed to snap suddenly from his bemused state. "Suredly. Yet these designations have something in common. What, the Na?"

" 'Jackson' designation is what is called *family name*. Among the vivipars of Current Project Four, *family name* denotes egg-cluster, the Na believes—although this has not been his special area of training, he is ever alert for more data—whereas among those of Current Project Five—in which the Na has been specially trained—the first syllable indicates specific dam, the last syllable indicates the sire, and the intermediate syllable is a specific identity-assertive particle of no significance."

Arrettagorretta showed no surprise at the curious fact that the vivipars thus perpetuated a record of the specific dam; probably he knew it already and was merely testing. It was well that the Na had studied so assiduously. Much prestige attached to him already in the swarm-house, and he had already placed his graffitti many times over those of other Nas whose training had been in less prestigious areas. Later, at food-taking, he would tell of this interview, he would demonstrate how he had eaten for the 'Gorretta-Sire, no one could protest his using his hands to take food under the circumstances. How the other Nas would look at him with low-nest envy!

And also and much more important: the impressed looks of the young Ma who stood opposite from him at food-taking—and the other young Mas, the non-dams, not yet taken to nest!

At the thought of this, the Na 14 'Parranto 600 began to tingle, and actually moved a bit in his excitement. Shocked into awareness, he immediately fell still once more, heard the Sire's voice droning on and on. He obliged himself to listen intently. Sooner or later something of importance would be said, and it was important that the Na should understand and remember it. It was very important, indeed, if his plans, his great, great plans, for himself were ever to become more than fantasies.

Arrettagorretta's instructions were delivered almost by rote, so infinitely often had he done it. But now, as sometimes, he became aware of a sense of rising urgency which made it necessary to concentrate on his words more than he was accustomed to.

". . . thus, after indoctrination into the manners of the vivipars of the Project Areas, comes training in negotiating the many-pathed ways. You must avoid those which lead into death-worlds, into worlds unsuitable for Chulpex by reason of climate or atmosphere or mass or hostile molecular make-up or such similar reasons; also those sociologically unsuitable; also those of Canceled Projects. Empty areas would be of course the best, empty of higher life-forms. But these are rare, few have ever been located, in every case attempts at penetration have been obliged to be abandoned. Moreover, they pose hypothetical dangers, as, thus: May it not be that they are empty of higher life because they are

basically unsuitable for higher life? Can it be said for certain
that higher life did not once exist there and subsequently die
out?

"Therefore, although empty areas would be theoretically
the best, a pragmatic approach requires evidence that Project
Areas have been tested by other higher life-forms, specifically
chulpechoid ones. And so—"

But the old urgency continued its familiar rise. And,
speaking the old, familiar words with a minimum of awareness, now he had determined that the urgency did not thence
arise, Arrettagorretta tried to analyze it. Hunger it was not,
he had taken sufficient food not long ago. Neither was it
cyclical necessity requiring relief via either breeding or anger-
outlet—although his mind paused to savor, briefly, the future
possibilities of both.

The vast room filled with charts was otherwise empty of
any but the Sire and the Na. Outside, he knew, the huge
complex was aswarm with life engaged into the endless tasks
of food-processing, maintenance and repair and salvage (particularly salvage). Deep, deep down, were the egg-clusters;
every multicycle there were more of them. And even deeper
were the great generators tapping the central heat of this
world; and every multicycle there was less of it.

Thence, the urgency. Having focalized it, the 'Gorretta-
Sire all but trembled, suppressing his desire to rise from his
dais and run roaring through the corridors and swarm-ways,
trampling upon the low-nest and ignorant life filling them, and
confront with his rage and fear and fury the other Sires.

But that was not the way. It made no more sense than it
would to destroy the egg-clusters—as Arrantoparranto had so
long and often suggested. To what end? Merely to extend
food supply another few score thousand multicycles? This
was not the victory, the life-through-life, which alone could
satisfy the sense of race urgency. Thus Arrettagorretta had
pointed out to him. And when the 'Parranto-Sire—so
anguished word was brought—had finally refused to breed,
Arrettagorretta had risen from his dais and summoned his
war-Nas and his work-Nas and marched upon the 'Parranto
and met no resistance and walled him up within his own
chamber under the sight of his own eyes.

And Arrantoparranto had neither moved nor uttered
sound.

Then Arrettagoretta caused another great chamber to be
made ready and summoned into him all the 'Parranto-Mas
ready for breeding and had bred with them and told them off

into cluster-groups and after that all went as was usual and was proper.

Sireship among the Chulpex was neither hereditary nor elective. It was occupative.

Now the last of the 'Parranto get was coming into full maturity. The pressing Projects must go on, must go on, and on and on, until the proper way of assuring life-through-life was found, and the infinite continuation of the race assured.

". . . strange and alien though the ways of the vivipars are, yet they must be mastered. Distorted though their patterns of logic are, yet they must, whenever possible, be followed. Else the race will die, the Na. The race will die."

There were natural chambers in the rocky strata of at least one subsection of Current Project Area Four, and the Na 14 'Parranto 600 thought about them even as he ventured to break the silence. "Success is certainly assured, the Na," he said, in his most respectful tones, "not only because of his special training but most assuredly because of the information and instruction he has been privileged to hear from the Sire to whose swarm he has been subsumed."

And he would say to the young Na, while she was awed and impressed at hearing of his interview and seeing him eat with his hands, "Is it not that the Na is being trained to become himself a sire? Suredly—and in the new place which he will find he shall prove his potency and the dams of his egg-clusters will be all of a most superior type—such as the young Ma who stands near him now at food-taking."

And she—

"Success is not at all assured," the 'Gorretta-Sire declared. "I am grown old and huge and have lost count of the multi-cycles, and in all this time we have tried and we have tried and we have yet to be making a successful penetration of the many-pathed ways. 'Success!' What is 'success?' Is it merely to master one vivipar or even one hundred vivipars? Is the Na still wet from his egg-sac to talk of such idiocy?"

Cringing and keening, the Na waited till the unexpected display of emotion ceased; then whined that he had been furnished with inadequate information. But he was far from being really dismayed. Now and then the sires behaved so; it was their privilege; and when he, the Na, was himself a sire, he, too, would behave so. But, actually, what was the problem? The area of Current Project Four was satisfactory in regard to climate and atmosphere and mass and it was still a young world and it had a chulpechoid population intelligent enough to be useful as long as was necessary and small enough in number to be easily controlled.

And the name of it, not that this was important, was Red Fish Land.

Having returned from the great sire-chamber to take some rest on the 600 shelf, the Na reflected on his planned conversation in the familiar damp and chill, the familiar scent of his cluster-sibs. He considered getting down and placing more graffitti, but it was even more pleasant to continue lying and planning. Later; he would do it later. He thought of all the ones even now reclining on the Ma shelf . . . young, yet mature; nubile, yet not yet available.

And, certainly, not yet available to *him*.

Not yet. Not here.

Presently, with one accord, all arose to go and take food. It was next that things began to go not rightly. To begin with, there were this time no solids among the food to be taken, and so he was obliged to mimic and demonstrate merely with empty-handed gestures how he took food in the presence of the 'Gorretta-Sire. With the result that the young Ma opposite him, like all the young Mas (and, for that matter, like all the other Mas), did not even look up from her feeding more than once.

Hastily, the Na 14 ceased talking and dipped his mouth into the food, lest he be deprived of his rightful share. But he ate faster so that he could soon commence speaking again.

"—then, having gone through to this new place—"

"How is the Na going through to this new place? Information is desired."

Breath-aura identified him as the Na 27, also of the 600 cluster. This was ever an assertive one, the Na 14 remembered with just the slightest trace of uneasiness. But, so—let the answer confuse and confound him: "The Na will proceed through the many-fold paths, as he has been trained."

A work-Na at the foot of the table paused and looked up, impressed, food dripping from his pale, oval face. The Na 14 quickly repeated the mime of eating with his hands. The work-Na gaped and grunted.

But the Na 27 seemed neither confused nor confounded. "Oh, thus," he said. "And the obstacles?"

"Obstacles? What obstacles?"

The Na 27 derided loudly, causing others to look up. " 'What obstacles?' " he repeated, next. "Obviously training for the Na is far from complete. He knows nothing of those who watch and those who guard and those who fight; monsters and menaces; yet the Na thinks so easily to proceed through the many-fold paths. This is ignorance, this is quite low-nest." And again he derided.

The Na felt fury rising. He had after all achieved no prestige as he meant to; worse, he had made himself ridiculous. How to escape? It was at this moment that the work-Na at the foot of the table, his mind working slowly, unwisely contributed to the derision. Such opportunities seldom came the way of his kind and he was unable to resist.

Instantly the Na 14 flung out his left upper arm and pointed. "It is grown old, the work-Na! See! See how opaque his body! Old! Old! It cannot do a full stint's work, yet it comes nonetheless to take food! Go, old one, and die!"

Mouth open in stunned, wordless protest, the work-Na produced a feeble squeak as all turned to look at him. Then they turned back, those near crowding him from the food. Once, twice, it hopped up the line at the table, then down the line, but none would give space. So the old Na turned and went back to its place on the resting shelf and lay down to die.

The others ate on hastily and did not look up again and the Na 14 felt his fury somewhat subsiding.

Afterward was the pause for digestion, then from every comb-hole in the swarm-house the occupants poured forth to their tasks. The young Ma was bound for the clusters, there to watch for the coming forth of the fry, to lick them dry and do the other things requisite to prepare them for the nursery. The Na moved quickly to walk beside her through the throng.

"Would you not like to be a prime dam to a new sire in a new place?"

She did not choose to reply obliquely, to regard this as a hypothetical question. "You are only a Na," she said, "not a sire."

"I shall be! I shall be a sire!"

"You are small. Sires are big."

"They *become* big," he said, excitedly. "Sires may eat much protein and as they grow older, they—"

"The Na delays me from reaching my tasks promptly," she said, and, quickening her step, hastened away from him. She was right; the Na turned hastily toward his training-place. But his thoughts were far from thence. Dim, they were, yet infinitely desirable; inchoate for the most part, at best scarcely formed. Strange, new thoughts, hot and frightening and unspeakably exciting. Let the young Ma go to her routine and humble tasks, content to await the summons to the established Sire and to remain but a number in a stud-book. The Na did not need her, the Na could wait, the Na had other thoughts on the subject. Let her go tend the clusters. There were, after all, always plenty of clusters.

There were always enough eggs.

Unlike the Sire, the instructor-Na did not confuse Current Projects Four and Five. Possibly this was because, unlike the Sire, he had never heard of any but the one he was assigned to. Instructors tended to be very single-minded; if he had heard, he would have designedly forgotten it.

The other trainees had already begun to don the accoutrements when the Na scuttled in. The instructor eyed him and his silence did not for a moment make the latecomer think that this failure would not be recorded. Hastily he placed his lower, thinner arms to his body and let them follow the folds and curves so as best to diminish the protrusion from the basic lines of the torso. Then with his upper arms he bound the lower ones with the long strip of the thin flexible material from which the other accoutrements were made.

"Generally speaking," the instructor-Na intoned, "the higher vivipars of this area tend at all times to shield their bodies with these and similar accoutrements. Reasons to explain this are obscure. Vivipars have said it is because of heat; conversely, they have said it is because of cold. Innumerable are the inconsistencies of the vivipars, primitive life-forms which must give way to superior ones."

The trainee-Nas with much less difficulty than earlier had now completed decking and cloaking themselves, and sat upon a sort of detached shelf raised on legs.

"Whatever the reason for this cumbersome practice," the instructor continued, "it is obviously of infinite use to the Chulpex. The importance of it cannot be overstated. Therefore, we must consider the exceptions to it. The vivipars sometimes remove their coverings, it seems, in the presence of their own mates. As mating between us is physically impossible, such situations will not arise. Also, they have been known to remove them when they rest. To avoid this it may be necessary to explain that you are too hot, or, conversely, too cold. The last likely situation concerns the fact that, because of their primitive metabolisms, they frequently grow unclean and find it essential to wash their bodies in water; sometimes they immerse themselves in it. It has been observed that on such occasions, particularly in the absence of members of an opposite sex, they uncover themselves—sometimes completely, sometimes partially. The Na 14 'Parranto 600, the Na 97 'Murriste 526, conjecture such a situation, and proceed."

The two played a rapid finger-game to see who took which role, and then enacted the necessary scene. It was well enough, the instructor said, when they had done; but he was not fully satisfied with their manipulation of the language. "It may not be wise to depend too fully on hypervocalization," he said. "We must have more drill on common speech. For this purpose the instructor-Na could desire an actual vivipar. The instructor-Na believes that on previous occasions actual vivipars were made available, and this possibility will be brought to the attention of those in charge. Admittedly the difficulties are great."

"The instructor-Na."

"The Na 14."

"Mention has been made of 'difficulties.' " Does this refer to the many-pathed way in general and in particular to those who watch and those who guard and those who fight—monsters and menaces?"

The other trainees looked at him in surprise and with some degree of uneasiness. The instructor-Na looked a longer while than was usual before speaking. Then he said, "The question will not be answered, for the reason that it refers to matters not yet reached by this training group. The instructor-Na is not pleased that the Na 14 presumes to bring up matters in advance of their proper place on the training schedule. All trainees will promptly erase this subject from their minds." He paused. "The instructor-Na has observed in the Na 14 tendencies toward an archaic and dangerous quality to which the ancients gave the name *personal ambition*. He informs the Na 14 that this quality might imperil the success of the Current Project."

Again he paused. "Further manifestations may result in the Na 14's being directed to cease to take food."

A slight, a very slight stir passed through the group. After a sufficient keening, the one addressed said, "It is regretted very much by the Na that he did not at once erase from his mind information improperly supplied him by the Na 27 'Parranto 600. He will do so immediately, appreciating the unparalleled excellence of the instruction being furnished his training group."

The instructor was mollified. They proceeded with speech drill. And when, subsequently, the Na 97 'Murristo 527 inquired of his former partner in vivipar miming what the purpose was of the latter's cluster-mate in improperly supplying him with information, the Na 14 answered that he did not understand the question.

In point of fact, he did understand it, for he had not erased the subject from his mind at all. It was fortunate that hypervocalization between Chulpex and Chulpex was impossible—as it seemed also to be between vivipar and vivipar. The Na intended henceforth to be most circumspect, to cease from giving evidence of identity-assertion as much as he could help. He was, after all, not yet a sire—he was still very far from even the proximate possibility. There were dangers in the many-pathed ways, then. This was true, the instructor-Na had as much as admitted it. Such being the case, it was well to avoid all dangers here at hand.

The Na was learning, he was learning fast, and by no means was his learning confined to matters on the instruction-schedule.

Arristemurriste did not follow the more-or-less solitary life favored by Arrettagorretta in the latter's chamber. Hence, it was by the agitated scurryings of his many attending-Nas that he first had notice of the latter's unprecedented approach. The days of Sire warring upon sire had long since passed; it was not for this that the war-Nas drilled and trained, although no doubt many of the tactics and maneuvers used dated back to the time when Chulpex lived on the world surface, when Sun Sarnis had not begun to cool, and it was not even unknown (so the records said) for swarm to fight swarm. Still, there were traces of protocol established in those hot, harsh days which still endured. As witness:

"The Sire, the Sire!"

"Why this commotion? Speak, informing me clearly and briefly."

"Arrettagorretta, the 'Gorretta-Sire, is approaching on our ramp!"

Not showing the astonishment he felt, he inquired in what state the other Sire was approaching—and was informed, slowly and alone.

" 'Slowly and alone . . .' Thus. When he reaches the summit of the ramp he will ask for my permission to proceed further. Inform those there that the permission is already accorded him. Prepare food, the Nas."

Wave after wave of 'Murriste Chulpex informed their Sire of his peer's progress. He had indulgently granted to all those adjacent to the other's route, who were not occupied in tasks of an emergency priority, consent to leave their duties and watch; for scarcely any of them had ever seen another sire before. When at last the vast bulk appeared in the great entrance-way of his chamber, he rose respectfully a trifle and greeted him.

"What, 'Gorretta, has word been brought you that I have refused to breed?"

Arrettagorretta paused in his approach. "Not so, 'Murriste. Assuredly it is not so."

"Assuredly not. I spoke in an exaggerated manner merely to indicate my surprise at your approach. Does not every Sire know that 'Gorretta never leaves his dais but to breed or to exercise anger-outlet, the only known exception in multi-cycles having been the misfortunate and unprecedented matter of the 'Parranto? Come, 'Gorretta, share my dais."

He rose on all sixes and moved to make way. "Not that even that was a complete exception, you having taken his Mas to nest. Why did you not share them among us?"

Ponderously the other Sire ascended to the dais and sank down upon it. At a gesture from his host, attending-Nas brought him food, and he took it. After a while he said, "It was designedly that I did not do so. I desired to express in a strong manner my abhorrence of the unnatural deed of the 'Parranto without utterly destroying the spirit of his swarms. . . . What reports have you? What new things?"

Arristemurriste gestured his Nas to withdraw a distance. Then he told his guest that all reports were more or less as might have been predicted. The continued loss of heat from the planetary core would require abandoning the two outer-most units and creating two new ones farther in toward the world's center, unless effective entrance was made to other worlds. Current Projects One and Two would probably have to be abandoned, and Three looked more and more dubious. And among the most recent hatch of his own get was a high proportion of females.

"Thus it is by all. I think, 'Murriste, that the new units require to be made larger than the ones they are to replace; also I see no other choice but that a certain number of under-lings pertaining to other units must be transferred to them in order to relieve pressure."

"That will not be necessary. Long before then, I am confident, we shall have achieved successful penetrations into Current Project Areas Four and Five."

Arrettagorretta made a swift, astonished gesture. "What thing is this? Did you not say that all reports were more or less what might have been predicted?"

"Thus. You have allowed yourself to be too much out of touch with things, 'Gorretta. It is not thus that life-through-life is to be perpetuated. But enough . . . it is not proper that one Sire should much reproach another. We must now consider the implications of such successful penetrations. In our own world, from our own inhabited areas, there is only one direction in which we can move: Inward. Downward. But the aquisition of the two Project Areas will give us mobility such as we have scarcely dared conjecture. They are thus to be valued not merely for themselves—rich, rich sources of space and heat and protein that they are—but for what they in turn can lead to—

"Infinite mobility, 'Gorretta! Crossroads after crossroads! It means that every Na now living is a potential sire!"

His guest moved and muttered. "They must not be told, yet. Almost I wish that I had not been told, myself. It will be difficult containing my impatience. Indeed, I can scarcely believe it—but I do not dare deny myself the hope. It has been long, 'Murriste . . . It has been so long . . ."

It would not be impossible to check the records to find out exactly how long, but that was not important. The only thing now of importance was victory. Escape. Penetration. Extension. Life! Life! And life-through-life!

Something roused the Na from deep rest. He looked without moving anything but his eyes, looked around and over the rows and rows of shelves where, from each silent and unmoving form arose a now-dim breath aura. All seemed as usual. Yet—he was certain—all was not quite as usual. He continued to look, and, meanwhile, he began to think. Rich, exciting, comforting were his thoughts. They were not unlike his often, earlier thoughts of the young Mas and of sireship; indeed, they included all of that . . . but they went much further. Surely no other Na had ever had such thoughts before.

Slowly his eyes moved from figure to figure and from shelf to shelf. And then he saw and then he realized what must have awakened him and all at once everything became clear to him.

Slowly and silently he extracted himself from his place on the shelf. Slowly and silently he moved through the dim, acrid-scented chill. There, there on the third shelf . . . a figure with an aura, a second, third, fourth figure, each with an aura . . . and a fifth figure—with no aura.

The body of the old work-Na was quite light and easily abstracted from its place without disturbing its neighbors. The Na considered dragging it, but decided against this because of the sound, no matter how slight, which this would make. Easily, then, he draped it over his shoulder and moved away. Someone had to do this task; it was in theory anyone's task, yet specifically it was no one's assigned task. The absence of the body would create neither surprise nor comment.

Through room after room, chamber after chamber, hole after hole, the Na proceeded; and came eventually to a deeply sloping way. The nature of the air, its temperature, scent, humidity, all began to change. And then something moved ahead.

It was an old work-Ma, blinking, frail, opaque. Plainly, the other Mas on duty here had been long delinquent in denying her access to food. However, this was beside the present point.

"Ah, food," she said. "This is well, the Na. It is long since enough food has been supplied. Although what you bring is not of the best. When the 'Parranto-Sire was still accessible there was more food. The Ma was then a dam and—"

She ceased her babbling and tugged at his burden. It scarcely moved.

"I will help the Ma."

"That is well and proper, the Na. The Ma is fully capable of doing her stint, indeed, more, for she requires less rest than the younger, slothful Mas. Nevertheless it is well."

She kept a hand on it as she moved ahead, but little more. "The Ma will also guide the Na. Thus. Thus. Further on. Through here. Thus. Down. Ahead. Here begin the clusters. Be careful, the Na. Directly down the center, faltering neither to the right nor the left, and on no account brushing against the clusters, lest eggs adhere. Thus."

The chittering of newly hatched and hungry fry feeding was still in the Na's mind when he returned at last to his place on the shelf. But there was so much in his mind that it did not dwell on inconsequential details.

He had merely to do this again when he was ready. Merely to bring another body for the fry. Merely to move slightly to the left or the right as he passed through the clusters. The few adhering eggs could be in an instant transferred to and scraped off on an inconspicuous place in his body. This he would do during the deep rest period just before his departure for the many-pathed way. The exposure to his own body warmth could not, dared not, be long maintained, of course. But it need not be. Once among the vivipars called the Red Fish People, he the Na, would seek out immediately one of the natural chambers in the upper sub-surface rock, and transfer the eggs.

And in time they would hatch and he would bring them food and as soon as the sex of the fry could be determined he would destroy all the males.

And all the females would grow to become Mas and dams and of them and to them he would be the Sire—the Sire!—he would be the *only* Sire!

And need never return to the world of the Chulpex at all . . .

There seemed to him, as he emerged reluctantly from these thoughts and before he sank again into deep rest, to be a minor uncertainty, not quite a flaw. He sought for it. He found it. In order to bring another body for the fry he would need another body. Could he depend on the timely death of another old work-Na? No. No, he could not. It would be absurd to do so.

The question of the source of a body, therefore, had for the present to remain unanswered. The Na did not let the hiatus bother him. For the moment the matter had to remain in abeyance.

As he let himself drift off into deep rest his eyes once more roved and roamed around the shelves. The last thing he remembered was looking long and without disquiet at the breath aura of the Na 27 'Parranto 600.

CHAPTER THREE

Joseph Bellamy rose from his desk and started for the fireplace, but a sudden pain made him wince and slump over. After a moment he straightened up, and stood considering what medicine he ought to take. He had, after all, a fairly wide choice. After settling on two tiny pills and one medium-sized capsule, and washing them down with a glass of well water, he continued on to the fireplace. It was late, the fire was beginning to ebb, and fetching and placing the great slabs of soft coal was a task beyond him. Already the large room had grown chill, away from the fire. He would move soon enough.

For now, though, all he wanted was right there in the great baronial hearth. A place for one was set out on the seat of a tall chair doing duty as table, chair facing one of the two taller, deeper, very high-backed benches which faced each other at right angles to the fire. Picking up an iron implement, Bellamy swung out to him the covered iron kettle which had hung close to the fire ever since it had been brought up from the kitchen by Keren at least an hour ago. Or perhaps it was more. His life was not one in which minor graduations of time counted for much, nor, for that matter, major ones.

The contents of the kettle were at about .50 on the scale running between soup and stew. Keren was a good cook, a rare thing (he understood, rather vaguely) in these days of things called TV dinners. Bellamy himself had never set eyes on either a TV dinner or the device which inspired it. He began to eat, slowly, and with small bites.

"Your name is Karen?" he had asked, that long, long ago day, his first at Darkglen.

"It is not," she said, sharply. "It's *Keren*. From the Bible."

"I don't—"

"Jemima, Keziah, and Keren-happuch, the three daughters of Job there, at his latter end, which the Lord blessed more than his beginning. Don't know that? You a heathen or something?"

No. No, he was not a heathen. No one held a deeper respect for the Great First Cause than he himself did. But not even Keren, good servant though she was, would stay on overnight any more—an any more dating back a good many years. Darkglen was too far away from anywhere in these times to keep overnight servants—not if they were enlisted from among local residents, anyway. They all had families and the families had no intention of living in servants' quarters on an isolated estate. From time to time the idea of hiring a foreign staff had occurred to him. But it was doubtful if foreign servants would long remain here in this vast anachronism of a house off in the deeps of the woods, either. Furthermore, he had grown used to being alone at night. The solitude of his prison was grown sweet to him.

He considered the clean lines of the chair in front of him. The 'People called Shakers' had made it—at least a century before. In a way they had been prisoners, too, although none of them, from Mother Ann Lee, who founded the order, on down, would have admitted that. They considered that their rule of communality and celibacy had set them all free from the prison of the flesh. They had long been numerous. Now they were reduced to a handful of ancient old women, living off the rents of the broad fields they were too feeble to till.

In a way, Bellamy considered, there was a certain parallel (he forced himself, ruthlessly, to consider it) between them and the Esquires of the Sword. For what were these last, nowadays, but a handful of old men? Sick, many of them, as he himself was. Grown rigid and ingrown, incapable of even holding their own, let alone expanding. Worse off, perhaps, because their particular vigil brought them no money. Worse off, perhaps, because the old Shakeresses, as they died off, did so in the serene content that they merely passed on to Heaven and that all remained well; whereas the thought that the Esquires of the Sword might die off, unreplaced, sent a chill into Bellamy which was not to be explained by the falling temperature of the room.

He came out of his reverie with a shiver which was more than half a shudder. Rising, he put on a sweater and an overcoat, loaded onto the wheeled cart (which had earlier brought kettle and supper setting from kitchen) his tray of medicines, books, and paper, and the two things called *ward* and *sword*, and pushed it out into and down the long hall.

There wasn't far to go. Five years ago he had given up his

old bedroom with the four-poster bed and fireplace only a
little less huge than the one in his office, and had had a
nearer, smaller room partitioned into a tiny two-room apartment for night use. He switched on the light. The original
ornate brass gas fixtures were still in place, but the tiny
gasworks behind the house, with its engine to convert gaso-
line into illuminating gas, had long since gone.

It had been chill in the chamber just quitted; here, it was
icy cold and his breath smoked. How often he had asked
Glory Smith (who, with Keren King and Ozzie Heid, consti-
tuted the total present year-round staff of Darkglen) to turn
on the electric heater here before she left. But the thought of
an hour's worth of electricity heating an empty room was
usually too much for Glory's thrifty soul to accept. And so,
having failed again to obey the order, she had primly climbed
into the back of Ozzie's old Chevrolet to be driven off to the
not-quite-village of Nokomas, where the two of them lived.

Lived apart, that is. That is, occupying two separate
houses. It was as common as any knowledge could be that
twice a week, when Glory's husband had gone off to the
poker game at the firehouse and Ozzie's daughter had gone
either to the movies or to choir practice, Ozzie and Glory
met for two hours of meta-connubial bliss. They didn't care.
By not sitting side by side in the car they made their gesture
toward the moralities. Everyone was satisfied.

Joseph Bellamy's life, freely chosen, after all, ruled out
concubinage as much as marriage. There was, he dimly remembered Charles Bellamy telling him, an Oriental Christian
church somewhere, whose patriarchate descended in the same
family from uncle to nephew. It did not, could not, descend
from father to son because the patriarch was allowed no
wife. Still, he—the patriarch, whoever he was—had an entire
church behind him; his duties could be publicly performed
. . . and publicly supported.

"You've had your college education," Charles Bellamy
said, on the same occasion, "and your year abroad. What do
you think of doing next?"

Joseph knew well that this was no casual question, no
casual meeting. Charles had paid for both college and tour as
he had paid for prep school before then. As—for that matter—he had paid and was still paying for the total support of
his unambitious younger brother and the latter's wife and son
and several daughters. And so the nephew now wondered
what the "offer" was going to be—on which ladder was the
rung and the chance to work himself up? The woolen mills

in Massachussetts, the cotton lands in Arkansas, the smelters
in Colorado and Nevada?—and knew that the "offer" was a
command, wherever it led.

He had known almost from the beginning that someday
the bill would be presented . . . and that he would have to
honor it. Well, he had enjoyed it all well enough. And his
parents, though they might live long, would not live forever.
Maud, Mabel, and Meg would eventually find husbands. And
by that time, surely, the debt (it was measured in moral
obligations, not dollars) would be paid. He would be his own
man. Until then—

"*We live,*" said Menander, "*not as we will, but as we
may.*"

"What do you think of doing next?" Charles Bellamy
repeated. He was a bulky man, with a long, wintery face, and
a short grizzled beard. '

"I thought perhaps—"

"You thought 'perhaps'—then you don't know for sure
what your thought in the matter really is. Well, well. What
was the perhaps?"

Lamely, haltingly, the nephew had stammered something
about hoping that perhaps a place might be found for him in
one of the Bellamy enterprises. He came, finally, to a halt,
confused and embarrassed. Both feelings ebbed away into
something like surprise as he saw, he scarcely knew how, but
the certainty was there, that Uncle Charles understood him
and his thoughts even more clearly than he did himself. And
surprise was succeeded by a calm relief. There was no need
for pretense any more.

"Well, Joe . . ." said Uncle Charles, "I didn't really think
that you were going to tell me that you wanted to go back to
Paris and become an artist, or go back to New York and
become an actor, or go back to Harvard and become an
instructor, or even that you wanted to settle down to Philadelphia and take a job in a bank directed by the fathers of
some college friends of yours . . . or anything. . . . I
really had no doubts that you would see your duty and be
ready to do it. It isn't quite what you think it is—what am I
saying? '*Quite?*' Lord!"

This last, unexpected remark pushed Joe Bellamy out of
his assurance and into confusion again. But that didn't last
long. Uncle Charles clearly knew what Joe had had in mind,
and it wasn't immediately important that Joe no longer had
the least idea what Uncle Charles had in mind. There was a
certainty about the older man which induced calm. There

was that same certainty about the room and house and whole estate. Seen from the upper window, then, across the lawns which seemed to have been cut from green velvet by tailor's shears, the woods seemed quite far away. The woods had grown much closer since . . . and not just about this house. The woods had grown much closer, all around the world.

"The Bellamy enterprises don't need you, Joe. They don't need me, either. The secret of staying successfully wealthy nowadays has come to be a matter of finding the right men to keep the store for the storekeeper. Something called 'management,' Joe; if you haven't heard it before in this connection, don't bother to make a note of it, you'll hear of it in this connection again. No one man in these times could possibly be an authority on wool *and* cotton *and* copper and everything else the family money has been put in. . . .

"Things aren't the way they were when old Joash Bellamy would bring the *Amelia* into port and fill her up with whatever looked like a good buy and take her back to the old home port and unload her at his brother Ned's wharf and warehouse and fill her up with whatever was on hand for another cruise—if he felt like it—or go kill trout at Spikin' Duyvel if he felt like it, instead.

"They aren't the way they were when Ned's son Tom used to sit in the old three-story countinghouse on Wall Street, either.

"But there is one thing that *is* just the same as it was in my Grandfather Tom's day, though. And in old Captain Joash's day, too, and all the way back to the days of John Edward Bellamy. You know, I suppose, that he was the first of our line to live in America. You probably don't know that no record exists of how he came to America—do you? Or why? No. Of course you don't.

"I mentioned the word *duty* a little while ago. The Bellamys have had a duty, a singular duty, I might say—nothing to do with making money. But money is essential to the doing of it. . . ."

His cold eyes stared through his nephew and he appeared to have fallen into a kind of reverie. The day was warm, the noon meal heavy. When Joseph's head snapped up, some indefinable time later, he found the apology he had begun hastily to form was addressed to an empty chair. A little leather-bound book lay on the desk, facing his own chair, and on it was a note in Uncle Charles's writing. It said, in curt entirety, *Read this.*

Later that day, only one place was set for dinner ("Mr.

Charles will not be down tonight, sir. He asks you to excuse him.") and after dinner an unsealed envelope was set beside his coffee cup: actually, on a silver salver. It contained a list of people and places he, Joseph John Edward Bellamy was to visit, and an approximate time-schedule for the visiting. It allowed him, he noted, with mingled curiosity and resignation, approximately one year.

It was not till that year was almost over that nephew realized that he had on that day seen uncle for the last time.

It was over the coffee, the brandy, the dark cigar, that the little book was read; baffling from the very beginning on the age-speckled title page.

> *Relation of Sir Ezekiel Grimm, the Muggletonian, concerning a Daemon or Monster which appeared to him in the Night. Together with a Discourse on the Nature of a Garment which the said Apparition left behind him. And the full Text of a Sermon intituled Muggletonianism described, exposed, and refuted. Preached by Mr. Macdougal at the Scottish Free Presbyterian Chapel in Gold-beaters'-lane. Printed by Jno Piggott at the Old Blackamore's Head, Mitre Court, 1723*

The men (they were all men) on the list of visits came in a considerable variety of ages and shapes and types. As the year went on, though, Bellamy was able to observe certain features which they had in common. Had each been seen in a crowd, he might not have stood out; had all been met rapidly, nothing might have been noticed about any. Young Bellamy possessed perhaps not the keenest mind around, but with the powerful hint which consisted in their all being in some way connected with his older kinsman, he was not too long in noticing the signs. There was a certain chilliness about them, for one thing, a degree of tenseness, a kind of sublimated fatigue. They were inclined to be bookish, pale, and sedentary. And there was a . . . a something else, on which he was a long time settling.

He thought he had it, at one point, toward the end of the first quarter of his year's tour. Mr. Gottfried Schtoltz gave the impression of having made his money in beer or perhaps sausages—and of having conscientiously and frequently sampled his own goods in order to assure of their being wholesome. He was also given to grunting as a conversational aid. Schtoltz shook Joe's hand, giving it a distinctive and peculiar pressure, and holding it a moment. Then he released it.

"Mmpf. You haf no mother," he said.

"Why . . . yes . . . I do. Mother is very much alive. Why—?"

"I mean, you haf not travelt."

"On the contrary, I've traveled considerably."

Schtoltz ceased to speak in mysteries. "I mean," he said, slowly and distinctly, "you are nodt, mmph, a vreemazon."

"Oh. No."

"Your ungle iss a vreemazon."

To this Joe had nothing to say, except that he believed that this was so. His host made one or two remarks which seemed equal *non sequiturs,* then began to discourse on the duty which man as an individual owed to man as a race—remarks rather similar to those made by the few other men already visited. Then he turned the conversation to music and the phonograph. Was Mr. Joseph Bellamy fond of both? Mr. Joseph Bellamy had not given the matter much thought? He would do well, then (mmpf), to give it much thought— and to build up a collection of phonograph records of good music . . . one could grow tired of books, said Gottfried Schtoltz.

The subject (not phonography) came up again. And it came up again. Finally, more than a bit bemused by this whole enforced caravan, and determined to seize hold of the one bit of tangible evidence—something which could be measured and scrutinized—he paused to purchase a number of books, most of them embossed on the cover with the design of a compass and a square. He read them as his train sped across the plains, alternately impressed . . . amused . . . and, once again, confused. The aims of fraternity, philanthropy, benevolence, seemed certainly unobjectionable. The oaths, or, as they seemed to be called, *obligations,* with their frightful penalties of physical mutilation, appeared more in keeping with a gang of boys playing cowboys and Indians than with an organization supposedly dating back to Hiram, the Master Craftsman of Tyre (according to one view); or to the cult of the dying god (according to another).

"You are not a freemason, I take it," said Major Jack Gans, by and by, when the year was half over.

"I have begun to think about becoming one. People have asked me if I were one, but no one has actually asked me to become one."

"The craft does not solicit. It is solicited."

And so Joseph Bellamy solicited. And was sent, with a letter, to a man not on his uncle's list. A man not at all like

those who were—thus destroying Joe's theory that perhaps
another thing they had in common was an awareness of
belonging to the same society—a warm, hearty, outdoor sort
of man.

"Well, hey! Captain Jack asks me to make you a mason on
sight! Yes, I can do it, that's a Grand Master's privilege,
President Taft, you know, he was made a Mason on sight.
Moving around, are you?—and will join a regular lodge when
you settle down. *Not* a good enough reason, in my opinion—
generally speaking. But—Major Jack asks it, *that's* a good
enough reason. Known him, oh, for years. Don't know anyone who knows more about the Brethren and their history
than he does—more than I'd care to know, impression I used
to get."

And so it was done. No great illumination followed immediately therefrom. But it was as if a door, a great, sealed
door, of whose existence in a shadowed wall he had gradually become aware of, had opened . . . just a crack. Yet, the
crack continued to widen. And Elias Ashmole proved the
key.

From the very later Middle Ages when—all persiflage to the
contrary—the first mention of a "mysterie" (or a ceremony
conveying secrets) among stonemasons appeared, down to
the early Eighteenth Century, the freemasons or workers in
freestone had been just that: a sort of guild or union of
workers with stone. From the Eighteenth Century onward
the associations of "operative" masons had been no different
from any other associations of craftsmen; and the "mysterie"
had passed over into the masonic lodges known today, where
the members did not actually work with stone, but employed
an elaborate language of allegory drawn from that work and
intended to teach a variety of moral truths.

The link, the bridge, was Elias Ashmole.

Before him, the *ancients*. After him, the *moderns*. But in
him, both. Before him, too, the world so little changed from
the days of Justinian; after him, the world which would
never cease changing. He was born into the realm ruled by
the mystical priest-king by divine right; he died in the world
ruled by Newtonian law and logic. All of this his quick,
keen, and supple mind had clearly grasped: and it was not
likely that it had failed to grasp the implications contained in
the primitive and disorganized freemasonry of his day. It was
not till a generation after his death that the first grand lodge

of freemasons was organized; after that, the old ways were gone forever.

It seemed though that somehow the ground had been prepared: for scarcely had the form of organized, official freemasonry with its established ritual and its three degrees, come formally into existence, when a host of other forms sprang, so it seemed, from nowhere . . . from the air . . . from the ground . . . Masonry in all forms proliferated like yeasts. Popes proscribed it. Kings suppressed it. In the clamor and the controversy little distinction was made between genuine and fraudulent, "regular" and "irregular," and "fraudulent" and "clandestine" forms; by the time some of the smoke had cleared away (it hadn't happened, even yet, that the scene was completely clear)—by that time some of the "clandestine" and "irregular" forms had become "regular" and "official." Others never had. Some vanished forever; some went underground.

An example of masonry unrecognized, even at first attacked, by official freemasonry, which later made good and found a place for itself alongside the older form, was the so-called Scottish Rite. Its well-organized pyramid of thirty-three degrees had developed out of a much larger number of independent degrees: but the first three degrees of Entered Apprentice, Fellow Craft, and Master Mason were not "worked" in the Scottish Rite. One first had to go up through these in the so-called York Rite of the Grand Lodges. Equally independent was the Royal Arch, and the entire system of the nights Templars, as well as such groups as the Shriners: not part of the basic system of freemasonry; one had still to have gone through the basic system before being able to go through the others.

And what others! Multitudes of them, with ornate titles, and a variety of purposes. Some were almost Byzantinely Christian, others were vehemently supradenominational; some were militantly antimonarchial, others were themselves headed by monarchs . . . So it went.

"Prior to the formation of the first grand lodge, certain trusted friends of Elias Ashmole had been making masons and passing on not only the mason word but a certain tradition which he, Elias, had told and taught them. After the formation of the first grand lodge, between 1717 and 1719, these same decided that henceforth they would make no more masons, but would take in only such as had been made masons according to the rules of the grand lodge," said a certain Mr. Eric Wiedemyer to Joseph Bellamy.

"And . . . this 'certain tradition'?"

"That—in modern terms—they continued to work as a sort of side degree. And, during the period not long after, when a lot of French . . . old French . . . pseudo-French . . . crept in all over masonry, this group adopted the name of Esquires Eslu, or, Elu, or Elected, do you see? of Esquires Eslu of the Sword. It cannot be said that this degree is either irregular or clandestine, as those two words are known in masonry; but it is not worked publicly. As a matter of fact," said Mr. Edward Wiedemyer, carefully, looking closely at Joseph Bellamy, "it is not known publicly that it still exists. . . . Do you understand?"

"And my uncle belonged to it? And all the others on his list, the ones I've been visiting, they all belong to it? And you as well?"

"To all your questions: Yes."

The young man gave a melancholy smile. "There is something almost ritualistic in the way that I am gradually being led into membership myself. Well, well. Very well. If my uncle and his friends and you are all members and sharers in the secret tradition of Elias Ashmole, then I am content . . . indeed: flattered . . . to become a member myself. At any time and in any place named."

And then he learned that more than mere membership was involved. That he would, if he joined, spend his whole life until replaced and released, in a Vigil comparable in some ways to the vigils of certain religious orders. On watch, forever on watch. On guard, perpetually on guard. Accepting a duty on behalf of and because of the whole human race. One which could not yet and perhaps never could, and certainly not in his lifetime, be revealed to the whole human race.

Bellamy slowly nodded. More and more, more and more, the figures of the pattern continued to fall into place.

"My post of duty . . . It would be, I suppose, at Darkglen? So I thought. Very well. I accept. I—I am not being presumptuous? I am to be accepted?"

"You have already been accepted, right worshipful compeer. An initiation will follow. But it will be no mere form. Come."

And he was taken and given the Obligation and shown the Gate into the Maze, and the ward which was the key to the Maze and the object called the Sword which was the guard of the Maze.

Concerning this last, he was told, "It isn't ornamental or

vestigeal, like the tiler's sword at a Blue Lodge meeting. It's functional. It disseminates . . . 'broadcasts' is a useful new word which might apply . . . it broadcasts what is known as *anger of a Sire*."

Bellamy repeated the phrase. Then, "What does that mean?" he asked. But Mr. Wiedemyer had already begun to speak of something else. "We—the Esquires, I mean—we've already had our inevitable schism. It occurred shortly after the Revolutionary War, when a General Frederick Flint broke away . . . was expelled, too: locking the barn door and all that. He set up his own organization, working their own degree and ritual. They adopted, as so many similar groups have done, a spurious title and a spurious history to go with it. Knights Lancers Elu of Livonia. Dropped from sight, more or less, but not from *our* sight, completely. However, membership seems largely confined to the Flint family. KLEL. Yes. Its original aims were not good.

"The Maze is not ours to use, do you see, compeer? We do not use it. We merely watch it. We were taught how. We serve . . . We serve."

CHAPTER FOUR

Nate Gordon pawed through the piles of manuscript on his work-table, a door-sized slab of mahogany-veneered something which served as desk. His practice was to make three copies of everything: a white-paper one for the magazine, a yellow second-sheet one for his files, and a blue-paper one just in case either of the others should get lost. Sometimes they got lost. Jamie Swift's innumerable young men assistant-apprentices were always loosing typescripts, filing a carnal account of a newly found lost tribe of white women in with the income-tax returns, for instance; or dispatching a practically stop-press report on the latest drag-races, not to the sports "book" in Chicago that was sweating for it, but to an imitation "Yank mag" in New Zealand which had ordered 3,000 words on Chicago gangsters. Jamie's young men tended to have their minds on other things than efficient agenting, and sooner or later he was reluctantly obliged to let them go, which permission they generally received with a good deal of sullen screaming, leaving poor Jamie so upset that he had to take the following day off ("I'm sah-ree," the answering service woman would explain to callers, "but Mister Swift is-int *in*, he's down with a virus—attending a stockholder's meeting —at the chiropodist's—voting—on jury duty—observing Yom Kippur—Reformation Day—the Vigil of St. Bridget of Sweden—I'm sah-ree, Mr. Swift is-int *in* today—"). Sometimes Lew Sharp, the editor of *Brute,* lost stories. Usually he lost them in The White Horse, The Cedar Bar, Stanley's, or similar humanitarian dispensaries on the seacoasts of Bohemia, whilst engaged with one of the Ivy League girls who descend upon the New York publishing industry like lemmings on a Lappish fjord. "See what you think of this one," he'd say, breathing like a drunken yoga and pulling any of the day's submissions at random from his ditty-case; "guy's got the um potentiality of being another Tom Wolfe, Christ you've got lovely eyes, only it seems to lack what I can't just quite put my finger on . . . You see what I mean? But let us not ruin those lovely eyes trying to read in this light, editors *live* by their eyes, Perri—Merri—Dixi—Domini—" or whatever the hell her name happened to be. As long as he got the girl up into his apartment, Lew didn't give a shit what happened to the typescript. It was replaceable. So Nathaniel Gordon pawed and pawed and pawed.

Somewhere in the mass and morass was a chapter and a half of a novel that he was looking for. He paused to read an item done on IBM Executive typeface, *From the desk of Sydney Sherman.* "Once again, as he is obliged too often to, Mr. Sherman finds it needful to draw contributors' attention to his very minimal standards for manuscript presentation. Mr. Sherman does not require manuscripts intended for his establishment to be engraved in copperplate on cream-laid paper with deckled edges; although such items are admittedly pleasant to receive, Mr. Sherman has not received any since he left the staff of *Delineator* late in the Coolidge Era. However, he draws the line and will continue to do so at items typed single-spaced with a red ribbon, on yellow or orange or blue construction paper, particularly when it is a *worn* red ribbon. Mr. Sherman also objects to MSS. mailed rolled up, as they require four hands to hold them flat and Mr. Sherman only has two—much as this may surprise such contributors. He did indeed at one time employ a chimpanzee to scrutinize such MSS., but it was found that the animal lacked editorial discernment, and it was persuaded to take a civil service appointment at the information window of the Main Post Office instead. Stories and articles, cobbled together with paper clips, Scotch or Irish or bicycle tape, surgical sutures, or even wholesome old-fashioned library paste, meet with a gentle but a rather unenthusiastic reception from Mr. Sherman. He wishes this were more widely known. Mr. Sherman is a devout supporter of the United Nations, and it is a source of much anguish to him that he is unable to retype and translate MSS. inflicted by threshing machines on extra-thin onionskin paper, well as he understands how high the postal rates are from Catalonia and Bhutan. He hopes that this inability will not cause political unrest in such renascent nations, for whom he will continue to entertain the highest regards, you should know. During the years 1919 and 1920 Mr. Sherman frequently took off his hat as parades dedicated to the cause of female franchise passed by, and he sincerely trusts that his positive refusal to peruse MSS. on which the baby has wee-weed or the childrens' luncheon jam been dropped will not incite supporters of the suffrage movement to place bombs in his mailbox or—" Nate dropped this and continued to shuffle the papers on his desk.

One of his problems seemed to be a growing disorganization of his professional life. Whereas formerly his working day had consisted of five hours of utter togetherness between himself and his typewriter, broken only by occasional trips to the bathroom; followed by a few hours of proofing and correction, note-making regarding the next day's work, and jotting down of notions for future articles; and at the stroke of five he covered his typewriter, tidied his desk, stacked the outgoing mail, and prepared to go down and celebrate the cocktail hour—but no longer.

Habit or inertia was still strong enough to carry him through a few paragraphs beginning, *"The drums of the drug-Crazed dervishes of Marakesh were getting pretty damned loud now as they approached the stinking hut where I was hidden in the harem of Ibn al-Idd with his half-naked houri, Farina—"* but after that things slowed down to a semicolon. Crocodiles continued to lay submerged with only their wicked little eyes showing above the water, and mass gang-bangs in the Sunda Seas never got past the *"Tuan, tonight full moon, more better you and Men take boat and go quick"* stage. He could tell the hawk from the handsaw now, and both were turning rusty . . . or something.

After a few futile hours of this, he would arise now and

make a cup of coffee or tea and ease his fundament and then sit down again, resolved to try good stuff. It is traditional to say that first novels are traditionally autobiographical—though tradition is silent concerning first novels in which the protagonist solves series of murders, which baffle the fuzz, or takes off in his patent spaceship for Proxima Centauri—so Nate dutifully considered novelizable elements in his own background. His paternal grandmother, he reflected, used to go away once a year for two weeks in Bermuda (whatever became of Bermuda?), and this event invariably produced in his mother, who had never been farther offshore than the Philadelphia ferryboat, symptoms of incipient hysteria; the result always being that Nate and his older brother Jerry were packed off to an aunt in Passaic, N.J., regarded by them as the boundary of the known world; and there they once saw a muskrat—or, at any rate a rat . . . What next? he asked himself, hunched over the mill. Sex, sexual initiation, supposedly either (a) squalid, or (b) glorious. Well. Actually, it had taken place next door on a well-made bed, and lasted about 35 seconds, Greenwich Meridian Time: "*That* wasn't very zonky, *was* it?" the girl said. And, "I must remember not to believe everything I read . . . not on the *floor*, for Heaven's sake! In the *toilet!*"

Nate sighed.

He had been in college and out of college, in the army and out of the army, now he was in love and even if he was to be out of love, still, it wouldn't be the same. Peggy was, in this case, just the trigger, the catalyst. He fumbled in his files, came out with a little piece about the Chinese New Year's Celebration in (of all places!) Chinatown. The paper dragons, he had realized, were actually paper lions, and were toted about by teen-aged boys who took turns and used a distinctive jerky sort of motion. He never found out what this was supposed to mean, but it seemed that a tradition carried on by kids and not old people was not likely to be dying off . . . There was more. It had a sort of nice, dry, observant feel to it. What was he going to do with it? He was still thinking in terms of *market*. This had no market, not as it was, not by N. Gordon, alias Pierce Taraval, Henry Dempsey, Jack Nydecker, Captain W. D. Lauterbach, etc. etc., and *sic* C. But it was sort of the thing he felt with increasing certainty that he would *like* to do—and do in Europe.

And there he came to that again, like a passenger on a train forever returning to the same station. Once in Europe, he would be, so he was sure, liberated to write what he wanted. But the money to get to Europe could only be gotten by writing what he didn't want—grammar or not. Almost, he thought, he could hold out long enough to raise the money, grind out the minimum number of articles—but not here. So, then, where? Not, certainly, even if he was sure where it currently was, at the home of his brother, Jerry, a cheerful tosspot who worked occasionally as a wool buyer. He'd never allow Nate to stay sober long enough. It was off season at all the beach resorts, but Nate would freeze to death at any place he could afford. No.

It had to be some place entirely different, some place not too far away, some place warmed or at least warmable, furnished—merely "furnishable" wouldn't do—some place he could fit into with a minimum of effort and cost, allowing him to use all his nervous energy to accomplish for the last time the writing he still needed and had come to loath. And Darkglen seemed to fit the description to a nicety.

Surprisingly, Jerry Gordon was still living at the same place and had still (or again) a connected telephone, and was home.

"Jerry? Nate."

"*Nate!*" —great good cheer. "I haven't got the money to lend you for an abortion, but, tell you what, I'll marry the girl for you instead, how's that?"

"Thanks a lot, but wait till you're asked. No, I called to ask you who Joseph Bellamy is? Didn't you once—"

He paused until there should have ceased the still recognizable and once very familiar sound of Jerry standing on his head and whistling *Dixie*, while the change and keys and pens and pencils and combs fell out of his pocket. Jerry, a trifle breathless, came back on the blower. "How's that, weanling? As long as I still can, I'm safe. Better than yoga and *lots* more fun than A.A. Jo-seph Bel-lamy. He isn't dead, is—? No, hey. Well, not that I wish him— He's not a bad old futz, but an old futz is really what he is. He's Aunt Mabel's brother. Remember Aunt Mabel? Six miles of hair and long mauve dresses? Before your time, I guess. Uncle Charley's wife, before they both went down on the *Titanic* or the *Lusitania* or was it a motorboat on Lake George.

"Anyway, Joe Bellamy has or had or has had more money than God and he lives in a house, if that's the precise word, cross between Penn Station and the Chateau Frontenac, designed by the Brothers Grimm, way the *Hell* off in the woods. And a couple of years ago he wrote me a letter like

something out of one of those old English novels where they
have girls and crusty old guardians, you know? Anyway, it
was all a fake, no pussy whatsoever, and he gave out with a
lot of mysterious hints or so it seemed to *me*, but meanwhile
there was all this great brandy up from the cellar and so I
got crocked. Naturally. And the next morning the manserv-
ant, or, to be precise, some local Kallikak that pushes the
lawn reaper around with his six-fingered hands, he drove me
down back to the station where I like to have froze my *balls*
off waiting for the train; why?"

Nate explained why, mentioned something of his present
problems, collected his brother's good wishes, declined to
make the trip to Darkglen via Jerry's apartment, and hung
up.

He understood what Jerry meant about the letter, if it was,
as it probably was, anything like the one he'd gotten himself,
it *did* seem faintly old English-novelish, with its references to
"family connections, which, while not close, are perhaps not
very distant," to Mr. Bellamy's interest in him "—though not
previously expressed," the "healthy, country air" around
Darkglen, "a house which some have found interesting . . .
hunting . . . terrain said to be good for skiing . . . a
quite large library . . ." and so on. City life tended to be
rather dull and often unpleasant at this time of year. Since
Mr. Nathaniel Gordon might, in view of his profession, be,
to a certain extent, master of his time and movement, etc.,
etc. . . .

At any rate, Mr. Bellamy invited him to visit Darkglen for
as long as he liked, with only the necessary warning that
social life there was nil and that he might find the company
of the master of Darkglen "neither exciting, nor, indeed, interesting." But he need have no more of that company than he
desired, for the guesthouse, "a cottage of ample but not
ungainly" size would be gotten ready for his stay.

Complicated instructions for reaching Darkglen by road
and by railroad followed. If Nate came the latter route,
Bellamy would arrange for transportation from the station;
as for notifying him, the service for which General Telephone charged outrageous fees was outrageously bad; but a
telegram "will almost invariably reach me, by one way or
another, within two days . . ."

"*I do indeed hope that you will accept,*" the letter concluded.

It seemed just the ticket. Doubtless Joe Bellamy *was* an
old futz, as Jerry Gordon had said; doubtless he would com-

plain about everything from the government to the fact that his children (if he had any) never came to visit him; but what the hell. At least he had enough savvy to appreciate that a younger guest would not want to be with him most of the time, and listening to his complaints an hour or two a day would be worth the opportunity Darkglen offered. For opportunity it was! New surroundings! Civilized comforts! Free room and board! Solitude! Yes, it was a great opportunity. Nate could write his ten (or twenty, depending on the word-lengths) set pieces at his own pace, unbugged, unbothered—when reaction set in, a brisk hike or even a dead run through the countryside—then to work again. In the evenings, the novel, if not entirely rapturous, experience of dinner at a large old country mansion, followed by a browse in the library for a book to go to sleep on.

In short, a stroke of luck, this letter was not to be passed up.

It had been years since Nate rode on any but a very few—in fact, one or two—main route trains, and the deterioration of service on the smaller, branch lines was an unpleasant surprise. The trains grew dirtier and later and older with each successive change . . . and four changes were involved. However, regarding the journey as (a) a fun thing in itself, and (b) practice for tripping and touring in Ruritania and Graustark, he was able to regard the worsening and the waits with equanimity. If the train was too hot, he took off his jacket and if it was too cold he put it back on, also his overcoat. He regretted most of all that the filthy-dirty windows prevented his observing most of the scenery. The railroads might still have to carry passengers, but they didn't have to let them look out at their own country. As for making available food and drink (except sometimes a trickle of dirty water), ha ha.

The final train was, as a baggage-smasher at the transfer point predicted, "some late." It was also the oldest, dirtiest, smelliest, most rust-eaten one of all. But it was the only game in town, so N. Gordon boarded it, and, after a gloomy, chilly, jerky ride, was let off at a goat shed in the snow-covered foothills. Fortunately, he was awaited.

"You, Mr. Jordan? I'm Ozzie Heid, work for Mr. Bellamy, let's get in the car. Lordy, it's cold out here, gimme your grip: there."

The warmth of the automobile was worth a mispronunciation, Nate thought; though the car seemed almost as old and

worn and untidy as the railroad coach, it seemed somehow
infinitely less nasty. The upthrusting springs of the front seat
were covered well enough with old blankets and sheepskins;
in the back, jammed with groceries and a pair of snowshoes
and a shotgun, an old red setter bitch helped a pile of winter
apples to mature.

"Long time since I picked up any visitor there at Fisho-
kan," Ozzie said, wiping the inside of the windshield. "Man
from the bank, doctor, and repairmen and such, they come
by car. Fellow of your name and about your general type
appearance, picked *him* up at the depot a few years ago, he
wasn't feeling no pain, like they say, stood on his head and
whistled *Dixie*, nice sparkly young fellow, didn't stay long,
though, mmmm, well . . ."

Ozzie's face resembled one of those bas-relief maps which
children are sometimes encouraged to make out of *papier-
mâché* or plaster or whatever it is, and then color, instead of
being taught to read and write and cypher, the little bastards;
there were ranges and ridges and riverine systems and coast-
lines and valleys, in a surprising variety of colors—red, white,
orange, yellow, purple. It seemed rather unfair to describe
him as a Kallikak and he had only five fingers on each
hand.

"That's Nokomas," he said, by and by, as they passed
through a cluster of old-looking houses dotted with new-
looking gas stations and a lunch-wagon; "that's where *we*
live, the people that work for Mr. Bellamy, used to be Nokomas *Mills,* first woolen mills in this here entire part of the
state, used water power, but that's all been done away with
now, oh, years and years ago. Next place we hit, Fisher's
Crossings, nothing but the roadhouse there and that's closed
this time of year, and the old Fisher house, after that, why,
just woods and hills till we get to Darkglen. Ought to make it
just about at dark, too. More or less I just unload you and
pick up Glory, that's Mrs. Smith, turn around and drive back
to home. Only body else that works there this time o' year,
that's Keren, she drives her own Buick."

"Drives it where?"

"Why, back to Nokomas, too—there, see there, that's where
my boy and me cut most our wood for this winter, I burn
wood, that's what I burn, *wood*. Takes us a lot of time to cut
enough cords, I can tell you, there's people who laugh at us,
got an oil burner, a person I could name, 'All I do is switch
a button,' he says. Yes, and come one good storm, down go
the wires, down goes the electricity, his oil tank might just be

a puddle of piss for all the good it does him, but I just go out
and get another armful of wood; here we turn off the county
road, *lie* down, Beauty, *lie* down. . . . Smells something in
the woods, dog has a nose that you wouldn't believe, she
used to cut up something wonderful at the big house from
time to time, seems to get terrible excited and then scared
half to death, so I don't bring her no more, except for just a
short trip like now."

Second-growth timber began to give way to thicker stands
of higher, older trees, and the land commenced rising more
steeply. It had been weeks since it had snowed in New York
City, and that fall had long since been churned into a greasy
black muck and washed away by rains. But here it still lay
"white and smooth and even"—or, Nate mused, was it "white
and *crisp* and even?"

The question was perhaps not so much why there were no
more such houses as Darkglen but why there ever had been.
They really had no natural source in the United States at all.
A case might be made for possible origins in the southern
"plantations" or the relatively fewer "manors" of the Hudson
Valley patroonships, but it could be a case only for the sake
of argument. No—the American country mansion did not
descend from anything, but neither was it original. It was
imitative, artificial, conspicuous construction, neither useful
nor ornamental, and often not even picturesquely ugly. No
owner of Darkglen or any of its fellows had ever cultivated
his fields for sustenance or even profit. It was one of the
examples of giganticism which so often herald the coming
extinction of a species, a great prostrate dinosaur of a house,
sprawled in the glade which had given it its name, neo-Tudor
out of mock-Gothic, with outbuildings wallowing about it
like whale calves.

"There she be," said Ozzie Heid. Nate interrupted his socio-
philosophizing to catch back at something Ozzie had answered earlier.

"You and Mrs. Smith drive back to Nokomas and so does
Mrs.—you mean, nobody stays here overnight but Mr. Bellamy?"

Ozzie braked to a stop beside a smaller phenotype of the
big house. "That's right, but we've got the guest place all
fixed up for you, it's nice and warm there."

It was, indeed, even though it smelled of recent cleaning
and of having been long closed up. The furniture was dark
and heavy and the lamp shades had *art nouveau* designs in
colored glass, the bathroom sink was marble—but it produced

hot water. Nate unpacked, looked around some more while the long tub filled, and then took a long, slow bath. After that he remembered his mother's warning about the danger of exposing himself to the cold air after a hot soak ("Your *pores* are open!") and, bundling up warmly, he went off to see for the first time the master of Darkglen.

Certainly he had never met anyone exactly like him before.

The difference lay in small things—he used a cocktail shaker—he had the dry, rather quiet, rather sexless look of an old, male librarian—the alert air of a hunter in the season of his chosen game—he quoted Paracelsus—his manner was old-fashioned, courteous, decisive—his skin seemed to show an inner unhealth as well as an outer pallor—and so on and on.

"You are fortunate in your profession," Mr. Bellamy said, as they drank their cocktails. "For one thing, it indicates . . . and I suppose it must tend to cultivate . . . the possession of inner resources, thus leaving you less dependent on the outer world for stimulus."

Nate said, "I hadn't thought about it that way." He at once began to think of it in that way, and this brought him back, of course, to the problems he had brought along with him.

"But it can happen . . . it has been known to happen . . . that a certain attention away from the outer world has brought forth an outward-turning which proves in the long run much richer."

Nate made a brief attempt to grapple with this statement, which his host had made rather intently, even leaning forward a bit; but it only made him think of monasteries, and this in turn made him wonder if he ought to visit any monasteries on his European trip . . . Mount Athos seemed always good for an article . . . if he ever got to make a European trip . . . perhaps he might do a piece out here . . . hmmm . . . Buddhist monasteries . . . *evil Buddhist monks,* the public might go for that just at the moment: Evil Buddhist Monks Tried to Burn Me Alive, *It all began one mad, marijuana-merry night in a Zen "coffeehouse" in*—

"—I don't know that the concepts of duty and of self-gratification are incompatible," Joseph Bellamy was saying, surveying the heavy glass held in his hand, "and—"

"—I don't, either," Nate replied, to the surprise of both.

Mr. Bellamy's expression lightened, brightened. "It came,

though, you know, as a slow surprise to me, that the highest
form of self-gratification could come about only through self-
fulfillment, and that duty could be the most certain path to
this . . . Eh?"

Nate said, "Mmm . . ."

Bellamy waited a moment, then he sat back, looked away
into the eye of the fire. It was a good, big fire tonight; his
young visitor made no work at all of feeding it. He might be
getting through to him, then, again, he absolutely might not;
they might have other things in mind altogether. Well. He
would not rush it. So far the approach was purely on the
level of philosophy and attitudes. Specifics and tangibles must
come later, if they came at all. He would not hurry. Either
this not-quite-kinsman of his would stay long enough . . .
for if he did not, if the loneliness overmastered him and
bore him away, then he was clearly not the man for the
work.

But, clearly, from the way he nursed his drink, he was not
a common drunkard like his older brother.

Bellamy after all could not know that Nate Gordon didn't
care for cocktails and was wondering if he might, should,
could, later on, try to put through a call to Peggy Stone in
New York. Or that one corner of Nate's mind was comforting itself with the safe recollection of a bottle of hundred-
proof rye in the valise in the guest house.

Word was brought to Et-dir-Mor that a great red fish, a
veritable mer-mother, was seen slowly making her way up
River Rahanarit, pausing to graze along the way in the shallow eel-meadows, lifting her head above water with increasing frequency, trying her long-unaccustomed lungs. The
gongs sounded slowly and the great drums beat with measured, signal pulse, and at each village the folk trooped down,
joyful and sedate, with flowers and festal bread to strew upon
the water. And as the signals resounded slowly over land and
water, the fen-men obediently removed all nets and stakes
and weirs and retreated to the thinlets where the red mother
would not go. For who knew in what marsh or estuary it
might please her at last to heave her great bulk from water
long enough to scour out a nest and—panting and whispering—deposit her clustering eggs.

Then she would ease her vast scarlet body back into the
channel and drift down-river to the sound of quick and
joyful bells and further offerings. But when the huge he-fish
made his own journey up along the river-road not a gong

would beat nor a drum sound, nor any offering be made, for the fish-fathers never ate at such times. Unfailingly, infallibly, he would find the nest and there do his own part, as no one watched. She was scarlet, he was crimson, she was huge, he was more huge. And as he in his own turn descended the river, from each riverine village one boat of chosen men would follow him until, as the great red mer-father disembogued into the bay, an entire procession of boats followed him, paddles flashing in the sun. Each group of six vessels would choose among its number by the odd-or-even paddle game, and then the choices would repeat this until one boat was selected.

And then the boatmen would draw lots.

At this time, and not before, was silence broken. The great shell-horns brayed and boo-boo'd from every boat. Thus they signaled the great red fish-father. Then, spread out now into a crescent formation, they approached, the winning boat apart and first, and in formal, fitting language, they challenged him.

If he withdrew, then, being excused, they mocked him and cursed him and covered him with scorn, and returned to the river in a fine bitter humor. Subsequently they would get drunk.

But if he chose to accept, if he turned for fight, then none but the fighting boat met him, the man of choice poised with his lances ready. One boat less might return to the river, or they might all return, towing the honored form of the great red fish behind the flotilla. They would honor him, praise him, mourn him, eat him.

Such was the nature of things; it was like wind and rain and sunlight and the acts of love and birth and dance.

Et-dir-Mor smiled when he heard that a red mer-mother was ascending River Rahanarit, the same warm smile with which he heard that a young man had been seen going off into the woods with one of his granddaughters. Life continued, the wheel turned, the earth moved, and even death—that delightful biological necessity—was an aspect of life. It delighted him to think how much he had to reflect upon this day: the appearance of a great red fish, a number of absolutely new mathematical problems sent him by the Council to be solved at his leisure, the promise shown as a Watcher by his twin grandsons—and, as always, the amusing speculation as to who their begetting father might have been! —and the promised visit of his old friend, Am-bir-Ros.

"I think I might cheer me by seeing the old mother," he

said, aloud. It was casually said, merely vocal expression of what, after all, was no more than a thought. But Ro-ved-Per was so immediately pleased at the notion of his grandfather having his pleasure that the thought became at once an intention, and so, a fact.

He looked at the flower-colored thing beneath his grandson's gaze. He pointed. "The lines . . . *here* . . . are, it seems to me, in more of a state of flux than usual. If you see any extension of that from the present level down along," his finger traced, "this group of lines, do, my daughter's son, send word to me directly."

"I will."

Et-dir-Mor pinned a light mantle over one shoulder and, going, turned only to ask, "Where is your twin? Is he studying?"

"No," said the young man, cheerfully; "copulating."

"Oh, that's nice . . . Still . . . He should study sometimes. One cannot always be copulating."

As he went out he heard Ro-ved-Per say, "One can—at *his* age!"

The High Physicist chuckled. Ro-der-Per was precisely six moments younger than his twin. So when the twin came romping in, singing and sweating and slapped him on the back and said something to him, he got up with no trace of visible senility. "Where is she?" he asked. "By the brook?"

"By the brook—go on, what are you waiting for? She won't take *root* there, you know!"

Ro-ved-Per nodded and hastened, swiveling around to point and say, "Watch those lines along you-know-where, grandfather says."

Ro-der-Per said he would. And he did. Then he recollected that he would be expected to have studied, when next he saw his grandfather. So he got up and looked for his book; not here, not there; never mind, he knew where it must be; he would just trot over for it and be back in a moment. And as it happened, fortunately, whilst trotting he met Nin-dar-Anna, and they stopped to talk about the coming of the fish-mother; she walked back with him as he went looking for his book, and eventually he found it. But . . . as his twin had remarked with the swift, thrusting accuracy of youth, "One can—at *his* age!"

He felt somewhat guilty at returning to his Watching later than he had expected, but when he looked at the ward, glittering lines and sparkling points, all seemed as before. He pursed his lips in a silent whistle, and, with one eye still on the stone, opened his book.

NNNonnggg . . . went the great bronze saucer-bell as Et-dir-Mor reached the river, and . . . *tuuummm* . . . went the huge drum-trunk. He concentrated on observing and naming by their proper, distinctive names, fifty-three shades of green in the foliage and the fields, hill, stream, sky, as he walked along; not including any which contained visible blue or visible yellow. It was one of the better days for this, clear air, although fifty-three was nothing much remarkable. His eye observed before he even subvocalized the fifty-fourth—the dress of the girl in the tiny cockle-craft not far offshore. She was calling something . . .

"*What?*"

". . . seen her? . . . you *seen* her?"

He had cupped his hands to shout that he had not yet seen any sign of the red mer-mother, when something else occupied his eyes and mind. It was but a flash in the middle distance, but he was trained to note such flashes, distant or near. His monocular was clapped to his better eye so swiftly it was almost like a reflex. And there he recognized it. No one else hereabouts might have, but to him it was unmistakable.

A Chulpex.

He knew it by its gait alone: torso tipped slightly forward, arms held slightly away from the sides. The untrained eye might never notice these things—unless, perhaps, it might see (most unlikely) several of the creatures together. Et-dir-Mor knew, too, what he would see when (or if) he drew close, the skin unnaturally white and always damp, "like humans who have been living under a rock for a long time," was the way Am-bir-Ros put it; the scant and colorless stringy hair; the voice flat and harsh and deep; the digit-nails unusually thick and yellow; the smell like rank earth. . . .

He knew as well the path it was hurrying along, which led to the hills, and he considered as he started off the quickest way of reaching it. The girl in the boat called again. Automatically, Et-dir-Mor turned, he saw her standing up, waving, but he couldn't tarry now to await the passing of the great red fish . . . *The silly child will fall if she's not careful,* he thought: she almost immediately did so. This meant no more than if she had tripped and fallen on the shore, for there was no one in Red Fish Land who was not able to swim. Still . . . he waited a moment . . . her head did not reappear . . .

Without drawing breath for a sigh, Et-dir-Mor ran to the banks, cast off his mantle, and dived in.

"A pretty little chitty," Am-bir-Ros said, stroking his white mustaches. He had picked up many Anglo-Indian expressions during his many years in England, and if he did not always use them correctly, it made no difference here. The girl was drying her long black hair in the soft sunlight of Et-dir-Mor's courtyard, chatting with the twins, showing no ill effects from having bumped her head on the boat.

"Yes," his host and friend said, in a considering tone. "Her bosom at this stage is interesting, though not—in my opinion—beautiful. One never knows how the dugs will develop."

The other old man frowned. "Don't be so damned clinical. Oh, well, who am I to criticize? Do you realize that there was a time, in my old time and country, when I favored adultery yet abhorred nudity?"

"I've never fully understood the concept of adultery. Your place of origin seems fascinating. Perhaps I may yet visit it."

"Don't. It's a dung heap, a cesspool, everything's the opposite from here. My sons, at that age, for instance, would be skulking around trying to get first shot at that girl, I'm sure—instead of waiting politely, as the twins are doing, for someone else to relieve them of the untidy task of defloration. Well. 'If youth knew, if age could.' And here, age doesn't have to want to 'could'. So you think one of those critters got past here, do you?"

Et-dir-Mor said that he was sure of it, had asked—but without making a great point of it—to be informed of any strangers observed. "Sooner or later he will give himself away. This time, I hope, without having caused much trouble. Ah, the things which pass along! It was when I was no older than the twins that I encountered on one path three levels off (how can one say *up* or *down* there?) perhaps the strangest sight of all: a man mounted upon an animal and both beast and rider were clothed in metal. He had something in his hand like a lance and he opened a window in his metal mask and—"

"You silly, six-fingered freak, you've told me that story half a hundred times! Oh, hey there! Another entry for the never-to-be-published New, Revised Edition of *The Devil's Dictionary*: FREAK. *A man who, in your world, has only ten fingers; in my world, one who has twelve.*" He got up, went over to the ward-stone, peered into it.

"I suppose," he said, slowly, "that in the hands of someone like Joseph Smith this could be an Urim and Thummim. It almost unsettled me forever, I can tell you, oh, not the stone, but coming through. I knew those Mexicans meant to shoot me for sure, I didn't care, it seemed just a damned stupid joke, a fitting end to what I'd always regarded as a damned stupid performance—life, I mean. There was another American there, never did learn his name, weeping and wailing till I got tired of it. So I walked away a bit to be by myself, thinking, 'All the Rebel bullets in creation couldn't get you, Brose, and now—'

"My first thought was that they'd shot me in the back and that it was the moment of my death, prolonged just enough for me to have delusions, like the hanged man in one of my stories, can't remember its name, doesn't matter. Then I came to realize that that couldn't be so, but I still didn't know what *was* so. It was dark and it shone with light. It wasn't anywhere and it led everywhere. It had its false heavens and its private hells. And then, finally, I came out here. By rights I ought to've died there on that hill from a Villista bullet. Still alive, though. Funny thing is, I don't mind that any more."

One of the twins had come in and was listening, preoccupiedly indulging in the typical gesture of running his palms along the smooth, sparse hair which covered the skin in all the males of his people. "If the experience changed you, Ambir-Ros," he said, "might it not change the Chulpex, too?"

Old Bierce shook his head. "It never has. It never will. It never can. Don't you see, boy, they aren't critters such as the rest of us. It isn't just a matter of their having different bodies or anything like that. They aren't just another little group using or wanting to use a fraction of the Maze and not aware of the Whole. They *are* aware, everything indicates it. But their attitude toward it can never be anything but an aberrant one, boy, because the world they come from ought not properly to be there at all. It's on an arm of the Maze that doesn't fit in with the rest. Look. Look there—"

Grandson and grandson followed his tracing finger. "Don't you see how it's different? Of course you do. It's an aberration, boy. It's an aberration. Just like a tumor is an aberration. And if it ever spreads—"

CHAPTER FIVE

Tas-tir-Hella was out hunting mushrooms in the hills. At least, so she said, and even partially convinced herself that this was so. She had a basket with her to put the mushrooms in, if she found any good ones; also in the basket was a lunch. This was what Am-bir-Ros might have called "the giveaway," because the lunch was ample enough for two, and Tas-tir-Hella had not that large an appetite.

At least, not for food.

However, she did *like* mushrooms, so, even if . . .

It was three months since she'd left the Observatory and it was another month before it would be time to go back. She had no particular preference for life in the Centra over life in the Villages, or the other way around, for that matter. Each had its own distinctive worth: in the Villages, no thousand player orchestras; in the Centra, no deep and leafy woods. The cool, slightly damp air was pleasant; here there were tiny pools and moss and ferns; here the honey-lizards did their mating dances, shimmering and iridescent and sounding like tiny bells. She kept her eyes open for ark trees, at the base of which the tasty little noars grew. Too, Tas-tir-Hella kept her eyes open for the spaces in between the tarra bushes, for here grew the big and meaty bondas.

But, for the most part, she just kept her eyes open. Her ears, too.

In such a mood she was, expectant, hopeful, well prepared for disappointment. She paused to consider an urge to go uphill against all her intentions of going downhill. It was rather a strong urge, and so, with a shrug, she decided to yield to it. Grayfowl generally frequented the glades and dells, but it was far from unusual for them to be found on the upper slopes. Besides, even hunters who favored grayfowl might take a notion to seek other game, upland game.

Her luck could hardly be worse than it had so far been.

She felt rather pleased on reaching the giant, towering, rounded rocks which seemed to burst like broken bones from the upper temples of the hills. It lacked the feeling of the wooded parts below but it seemed somehow encouraging, she could not say why; so she continued to climb. This was no place, certainly, for mushrooms, although . . . Tas-tir-Hella stopped a bit, frowning slightly, trying to follow the rest of the thought; then, suddenly, it came to her. Caves. No place for mushrooms, although there were . . . weren't there? . . . caves up here, and in some of them might be found the pale and coronet-shaped dwarthu, the smoky-tasting. Dwarthu were excellent, a good day's work if she could fill even the bottom of the basket with them.

Tas-tir-Hella felt a faint desire to damn all mushrooms, but it was faint.

She saw someone as she climbed over a smooth limb of rock, someone down below, a stranger. She little reckoned on just how very strange, though.

"We greet you, maiden," the stranger said, touching his mouth as he bowed. She stifled an inclination to smile at the archaic manner and address—indeed, the stranger's dress itself was archaic, swathed as he was in the darkest garments she had ever seen. Into her mind came lines from an old poem:

Black is his robe from crown to toe.
His flesh is white and warm below . . .

White, his flesh certainly was, almost as though he had been living in a cave himself for years. But . . . *warm?* No . . . warm, his flesh certainly did not look. However, she was not interested in his flesh. Not in his. "Our name is Ten-pid-Ar," he said.

"Mine is Tas-tir-Hella, and I think I should tell you that it's not the custom here, in our country, that is, to speak of one's self in the plural."

"The N— We— that is, I was not informed. I will remember," Ten-pid-Ar sounded startled for a moment; then the entire tenor of his voice changed, as he added, "I will reward you . . ."

This time she did smile, but it trailed away, for, somehow, the man from . . . wherever it was, it must be *far* . . .! —the man no longer seemed to be amusing. What then? Faintly frightening, stranger than merely strange, yet . . . impressive? . . . awesome? Well! What odd thoughts!

"Reward me for for what, Ten-pid-Ar? And how?"

He had seemed to slump forward just a trifle; now he quickly became erect. "For assisting me, a stranger. For assistance, also, yet to be given. Thus, for what. And how, the Tas-tir-Hella? This is how. With what you desire. I will give you Far-ven-Sul, he who hunts; I will give you the use of his body and—"

She cried out, "Oh, don't!" and turned aside her head, because she was suddenly certain that this was a cruel and elaborate joke; such acts were not common in Red Fish Land, indeed, they were scarcely known . . . known, though, and though she had thought no one would or could know, but known clearly: her hopeless and ridiculous lust for Far-ven-Sul—she who could easily be his mother and, almost, his grandmother. Someone must have noticed her covert looks, someone must have marked the very quickening of her breath as he passed by . . . someone . . . Who . . .? Who . . .?

Who was this pale stranger in black?

No, no, it was absurd even to think in passing of such old legends and folk tales: the joke was simply that: a joke. Who was engaged in the masquerade, she couldn't guess, but the whole thing—archaic greeting, costume, and all—must be part of some jest. Perhaps it was connected in some way with the celebrations attendant upon the coming up river of the great red she-fish. It was accident, that was all; it could only be by accident that her name and *his* name were coupled.

Still, it hurt. It still hurt.

"Very well." Tas-tir-Hella forced her face into a smile. "I have given you assistance, and you will give me Far-ven-Sul. Where is he?"

The directions were specific enough, by the sound of them. She shrugged, she followed them, her basket dangling from her limp, indifferent hand. It would be too bad, really, if Far-ven-Sul were also engaged in the joke. But she'd see it through . . . If the experience proved too painful, well, she could always return earlier to her Centra. Or even go somewhere else till that be time.

He was there, sitting on a rock, idling his weapon in his hand, and looked up, somewhat sullen, but not unfriendly, as she approached. Gesturing toward her basket, he said "What, found no mushrooms?" She shook her head, not speaking, realizing that even if this were a . . . a hoax . . . even if she were doomed to be a butt and a victim (though unable to guess why), she still felt the same toward him. His light brown hair fell into his dark brown eyes, and he brushed it away, impatient.

"No . . . No mushrooms."

"An unlucky day. No game, either. One would think it
would *be* a lucky day, though—wouldn't you? The mother-
fish, I mean." He gave an impatient exclamation, struck his
thigh. "The whole day wasted! And no game, that means no
meal. Curse!"

What difference did it make, hoax, joke, whatever—? She
was face to face with him, close to him, talking to him. Tas-
tir-Hella swallowed, held her breath, then said, cautiously
courteous, "I'm sorry we've both had bad luck—" (Bad
luck?!)—"But, you know, I always bring along more than I
need to eat. Look. You see?"

He ceased to be the petulant hunter, then, became altogether the young man with healthy appetite. Indeed, he gave
her a quick hug before they settled down to eat. She ate little
enough, excusing herself; but nothing was left in the basket
when they were through. Then they talked—Far-ven-Sul
talked; she listened, in a happy daze—talked of things of no
consequence. Finally, with some hesitation, he proposed that
they make love. He was sure that she had so many, such
more mature lovers—she would probably find him gauche.
Still . . . if she did not mind . . . it would make him
happy. . . .

It was not, after all, an unlucky day at all, really.

Afterward, feeling so euphoric that even mysteries made
no matter, she mentioned something (but only something) of
the stranger. Far-ven-Sul, stroking her relaxed body, assured
her that he had never seen the man, heard nothing of him.
"Sounds dull," he murmured. "Never mind about him . . ."

The stranger's final words to her, however, still were in her
ears. *Afterward, you will bring him to me, here.* In a way,
she was fearful of not complying. And in a way she felt
grateful. More—could she hope for more?—yes: she could
hope that it would not be ended and over soon, so—more.

"He isn't dull at all," she said. "And he . . . he has a
strange talent. Yes," she disengaged herself gently but continued to hold his hand, "I think we should go up there."

Afterward, in the waning daylight, Tas-tir-Hella and Far-
ven-Sul came down to the village in silence; she, happy
almost to serenity, but between the almost and the serenity
there was an uncertain, vague feeling which interposed itself
like a mountain between the sunlight and the plain. And he,
the hunter, hardly seemed to be aware of outer things, a
fierce and prideful hope burned in him, visible and hot.
When they saw ahead the first lights go on in the village, he
spoke up as though to himself. "He knew what it was that I

wanted, and I never spoke of it to anyone. I *know* that he knows, I *know* that I never spoke of it. This much I know, and so the rest I will believe. He asks very little, but if that's all he wants, I can do it. I know where there are such caves, no one else knows. And—and then—if he can arrange to do as he says—oh, if he can do that—"

His breath hissed, his breast rose, his hands moved. Then he became silent again.

When they came to the lane where she would turn off and he would not, Tas-tir-Hella touched his arm. "When shall we see each other again?"

He looked at her blankly. Then he said, partly amused, partly annoyed, "Because I ate from your basket once, must I eat from it forever? No . . . Laying is like lunching, and I can do it every day. Thanks," he added, carelessly, turning away, not seeing her shrink back as the dream turned to ashes. "There is only one thing that I *want,* and I must have it and I *will!*" he walked on, still talking as though to himself.

"And that is to be the one who kills the great red fish!"

Least, least, infinitely the least of all the cognate concerns which vexed Arrettagorretta was the reported disappearance of the Na 27 'Parranto 600. His absence had finally been explained—up to a point—by the discovery that he was not only dead but had been ingested by the young fry in the nursery. Piece by piece the evidence accumulated: an old work-Ma (much too old, she had since been directed to cease to take food), when questioned, reported that this was the second superfluous body brought in by the Na 14. The question of the previous one proved to be no question, it was of an old and superannuated work-Na who had died as properly directed.

But the report of the low-nest sweeper-Na was almost incredible, but, once credited, explained—though it did not excuse—the terror of the witness and his failure to report what he had seen until the massive search and questioning reached him in turn.

"The Na 14 placed two of his hands about the throat of the Na 27, having approached him from behind, following him when the latter arose in the night to ease himself. He, the Na 14, held him, the Na 27, with his other hands. The latter struggled a while and then ceased to do so." Such was the report of the witness, which had to be believed. But what reason could the Na 14 have had to commit an act for which there was not only no explanation, but not even a name? To destroy a fellow Chulpex as though he were some lower form of life?

The Na 14 himself could not be questioned, having departed on his mission along the many-pathed way. His having committed such an act raised an infinity of questions concerning the success of his mission and fitness for it, particularly since the act in question—the destruction of the Na 27—was committed during the long rest period the night before his departure. It was while musing on this that the ultimate report was brought Arrettagorretta.

He remained in silence, trying to make sense of it.

"The egg-count cannot have been mistaken . . ." It was half-statement, half-question, and the Chief Supervising Ma interpreted it as the latter.

"The count was made one hundred times and manually and mechanically," she replied. There was no mistake, clearly.

"It follows no logic," the 'Gorretta-Sire said, slowly aloud, "that eggs should be missing. Could they have not adhered to one or more of the attendants through carelessness."

Defensively, the Chief Supervising Ma said, "On very rare occasions this has happened, but it has always been accounted for. On no occasion has any such number, or even approaching it, adhered to an attendant through carelessness."

Sometimes, the Sire had found, in dealing with an illogical situation, that a seemingly-illogical approach might reveal the existent though not priorly apparent logic. "Had anyone passed through or into the hatcheries who had not been authorized to do so? Only an accurate reply," he cautioned, "can be of service."

The Ma hesitated. "An accurate answer can be given," she said, "only after defining the term itself. Precision and accuracy are not always—"

"Reply at once, the Ma! Who entered?"

"It is always authorized for any to enter, indeed, it is but duty, to bring food consisting of bodies which have ceased to contain life; therefore the entrance of the Na 14—"

The Na 14!

Instantly the great 'Gorretta-Sire perceived all, understanding that the Na 14 had destroyed his fellow in order to have a body whereby to gain entry to the hatcheries and that therefrom he had stolen the eggs immediately before his departure: and with what purpose? What possible purpose other than the hideous one of becoming himself a Sire, independent, ruling his own swarm, making his own terms . . . his own plans . . . his own conquests . . . indifferent! indifferent! to the needs, the terrible, urgent needs of all the great Chulpex race! He would never report back, even if capable! Not only had his training gone for nought, it might have gone only into making and raising up an enemy: the Na 14 'Parranto 600 would not only nevermore assist invasion, he might well at some future date lead an invasion of his own! He who has slain one, will he abstain from slaying many?

All, in one mind-searing second, this raced through the brain of the great 'Gorretta-Sire. Huge, immense, immediate, was his need for anger-outlet. With a roar that shook the charts upon the walls of his chamber, he leaped from his dais and tore the Ma in half; then, bellowing his rage and fear and grief, he hurled his vast body out into the corridors and, trampling and tearing all who failed to flee in time, he made his furious and frantic way to the pen where a sufficient number of the unfit and the superfluous were kept for just such moments.

At length, sated, recovered, he sent messages revealing the matter to all his fellow Sires. The conference which followed was long and troubled. It was entirely possible that the wretched Na 14 had failed to get through to his destination, in which case no danger need be feared that he and any swarm he might raise would ever retrace the incredible difficulties of the journey and mount an invasion of the Chulpex world. They might hope this to be the case—but if it were the case, they would be no better off. Happen what had, happen what might, again there had been a loss of time and time was as precious as life; indeed, it might be said that time *was* life.

Arristemurriste broke the silence. "It might be well that this has happened," he said. "It has shocked us from our accustomed thought patterns. A new thing has occurred, a new possibility has arisen, a new threat. Now, before we become accustomed to it and sink again into our old dull ways while the world continues to grow cold about us, let us consider a new plan.

"Everything must be changed, every emphasis placed upon breaking through. The number of mission groups, of trained agents, must be—not only doubled, tripled—but squared, cubed, increased again and again. Let the classrooms never be empty by day or by night. Pour forth our scouts until our swarm-houses sound to the echo of their emptiness. We can no longer wait.

"We cannot wait!"

"Let us consider the possibility," said King Wen, "that the Maze was not created in the past, but will be created in the future. As it occupies—and the verb, to occupy, is here used as a mere convenience—as it 'occupies' all time or is occupied by all time, this is possible."

Benjamin Bathurst shook his head. "This is not possible," he said, agreeably.

Enoch ben Jared said, "He is called *The Place,* for He is the place of the universe; but the universe is not His place. Surely it is but a commonplace, thus, to point out that He who is everywhere is also of necessity everywhen?—though is He bound to any necessity? only if He chooses to be— therefore He even now presides over the Last Judgment and even yet His spirit hovers over the face of the deep at First Beginning."

"It cannot be created henceforth," said Appolonius of Tyana, "for we are too near the end of time, near entropy. Unless we are correct in that time is infinitely divisible and therefore we ourselves will be and in fact already have been."

Caressing the muzzle of his bull, the Old Chap murmured that the secret of the Maze lay in its having no secret, the universe being in fact non-serial.

The Masters smiled at one another, and prepared to meditate calmly for an aeon or two.

But when the Chulpex Sires sent for the ward, living and pulsing fragment of the living and pulsing Maze, they learned that it, too, was gone. They had wondered how the Na 14 had dared. Now they knew. He had thought himself quite safe from pursuit, thus; he must have considered that he had climbed a height and pulled the ladder after him, or crossed a chasm and withdrawn the bridge. He surely believed he had left his Sires and fellows blind and stumbling, unable to know where he had gone, unable to follow.

"The blow is grievous," said Arristemurriste, in a muted voice.

But the 'Gorretta-Sire, calmed and refreshed by his anger-outlet, lifted an arm and pointed. "He has not taken the charts," 'Gorretta said. "He may have already passed onto ways which are not charted . . .

"Yet, again, he may not."

The conclusion, the decision, was obvious: The Na 14 had to be pursued, and with all power and with all haste.

As the vote concluded it was now Arrettagorretta who repeated the warning and the words. "We cannot wait. *We cannot wait.*"

CHAPTER SIX

Joseph Bellamy had said good night to his guest and now intended to take his ten o'clock medications and retire for the night himself. It was perhaps too early to tell what, if anything, he might expect from the young man . . . but the impressions seemed not unfavorable. Gordon appeared a serious and sober type, though inclined to be a bit vague on the precise nature of his writings. Not that Bellamy had been altogether precise, either. But that was not to be expected. One did not blurt out such a matter. One did not say—one *could* not say—I belong to a secret society, membership in which is limited to freemasons but which does not have any other connection with official or so-called "clandestine" freemasonry. One could not, at a first meeting and over cocktails or dinner or cigars and brandy, reveal that this secret society held in its hands the fate of humankind, which it guarded at great and terrible cost from greater and more terrible disaster. Not yet . . . Not yet . . .

Bellamy knew this as he knew his own name; yet his illness and his weariness and the knowledge that every year the average age of the Esquires of the Sword rose and that every year there were fewer of them—thus the burden increased while the bearers dwindled—made him repeat, unwittingly, the words of the Chulpex Sires: *"We cannot wait. We cannot wait."*

He took his medications and shuffled about the great, chill room gathering things together. He had glanced automatically at the ward-stone on entering; fortunately, all appeared well, no manifestations along the glowing lines of light required his attention. He hoped it would remain so at least until midnight, when his own watch ended, and that of

Ralph Wiedemyer began. He hoped, too, that Ralph's own health at least grew no worse. It should not, if loneliness was "a contributing factor" (cant phrase!), for Ralph lived and always had in a house full of family . . . family which knew only that "Uncle is a little bit . . . you know?—but perfectly harmless and really very nice: only he has to be left *alone* at nights; that's all . . ."

He looked out of the window, seeing that which he knew lay in the direction he looked, though he could not see it even in the daytime, not that it was all that far away in space. Geography rather than distance blocked what was a theoretically possible—should someone only clear away a range of low mountains and straighten out a river valley— view of the Flint lands. They, too, kept (at least Bellamy supposed they still kept) a Vigil, though a short-sighted and thoroughly selfish Vigil it was; had been since the days when General Flint, appropriately enough a friend of Colonel Burr, had broken with the Elected Esquires and founded his own degrees and order.

Once a year Bellamy received an investigator's report on the current Flint, a major in the militia or whatever they called it nowadays, or had been; but he had no great faith in it. What the man did in New York was hardly comparable in importance to what he did or hoped to do back there in the pitted hills behind Flint's Forge—although the report contained general references on this subject, too; Bellamy supposed the investigation firm had some yokel on their gratuities list—ah, well.

What had that last creature mumbled and whined at him? *Much old, much cold.* Yes, yes. And not just them, alone. *Much gold*: that was of course a lie, still, how often must that lie and others like it have been believed, legends of faërie gold which turned to ashes with the setting sun. And not that legend alone, no, the Chulpex were hardly pleasant or innocuous creatures, disliked from mere bigoted ignorance of their mores or folkways: faërie gold, what else? ghouls, ghosts, vampires. But—and this was a perpetual *but*—the Chulpexes were not the only, though they seemed the greatest, menace posed by the ever-guarded Maze. No—

Something flickered, something fled, moved like a fluid along a line on the "stone" surface of the ward, which changed color slightly but perceptibly. *So near!* And then he realized, with astonished horror, that the movement indicated was not on one of the usual lines. Automatically, he started for the "sword," the thin, thin thing with the short crossbar—

But of what use was that, *there*? It was then he felt again the warning in his chest, the sick and painful swelling of his heart. He had been cautioned. He dared not move. He dared not *not* move. If he should fail his trust, what might happen? And if he were to die—in *there*? Helplessly, his mind darted about. His eyes, too. The feeling of joy was like cool water on hot skin. Slowly, ever so slowly, he made his way, hands spread out like a blind man's, over to the table.

There, in the little plastic vial, were the tablets.

There, in the wall behind, was the signal.

He did not know which to do first. Perhaps he might manage to do both together.

Perhaps . . .

The sound, so faint and strange, at first made Nate Gordon think of sleigh bells. He paused, his pants half off, drew them on again, lit the lamp, went to the window, rubbed away the mist or frost, and peered out, holding his hand against the reflected light. But no cheery, picturesque Christmas-card scene of Pickwick types in a one-horse open cutter met his eyes. Nothing met his eyes except the frozen ground and, up and ahead, a light gleaming in the black hulk of Darkglen House. The sound ceased, began again, ended abruptly.

Nate pulled on the huge old bathrobe which had been provided him and went to the door. The wind blew chill in his face, but no one was there; as he looked about, shivering, he saw that there was no doorbell—just a knocker. He closed the door and considered. If the noise had not come from outside, then, it must have come from inside (unless someone was overhead in a balloon, ringing a hand bell). It had *seemed* like a bell. His glance went up— Sure enough. There, high up, was an old-fashioned electric bell-clapper. Even as he looked at it, a long loop of dusty matter detached itself and dropped silently to the floor. This, evidently, had muffled the sound and made it seem so curious and distant.

There was only one place the bell could have been rung, and that was in the main house; and it could mean only that he was for some reason wanted there. Nate dressed again, muffled and bundled himself up, took a quick shot from the bonded bottle, and trudged into the night.

It took several minutes of, first knocking, then pounding, then calling, at the side door he'd left by to convince him that no one was going to come and let him in. He deliberated a moment. The cold was numbing, and he wanted to return

to his cottage. But then the bell might ring again, and—
Besides, it was possible that something was wrong. The old
man might have fallen and broken a bone or something.
Nate shrugged and shivered and started trudging around the
outside of the house, looking for another way in. Salt crystals
crunched underfoot. Better that than snow to flounder in.
The windows of the house were too high up for him to
reach, and the basement windows were all shut tight. The
house had many doors, as was to be expected.

What was not to be expected was that one of them, low
down and opening upon a set of sunken steps, should be
wide open; or that upon the lowest step should be an incon-
gruous wad of steel wool.

Nate had lived long enough in Manhattan to recognize
this, jimmy-marks and the other signs of burglary. It was, he
realized, extremely unlikely, however, that here in the wilderness, miles and miles from bloody woof-woof, a Manhattan-
type burglar had jimmied open the door of Darkglen House
in hopes of snatching up a radio or a typewriter or a record
player to convert into quick fix-money.

And a country-house break-in implied a much bigger job
. . . and it implied, too, more than one man.

Swiftly, he considered. Loop around and look for the car
they must have come in and drive it away for help? No: the
car might be parked a mile away and have someone waiting
in it. Get upstairs as quickly as he could? For one thing, he
had no light, he could spend forever groping in the basement
looking for the stairs. Perhaps the best thing was to get back
to the guest cottage and have the operator get the nearest
police (state, probably) on the phone, and then ask *them*
what to do while he was waiting.

Half irresolute, he turned to go, turned back, the door
blew open a little bit more than it had been; and on the
ground, just before it swung back to where it had been, he
saw a pale little patch just about the size of a book of
matches. He stooped, groped, found it. That was what it
was.

Common sense told him never to mind the matches but go
on and carry out his program of calling for help. Slowly,
Nate shut the door behind him and, not so much ignoring
common sense as allowing it to wait a bit, he stood with his
back against the door and struck a match. As far as he could
see, advancing cautiously in the accompanying circle of
scant, pale light, the floor was clean and bare of obstacles.
The flame came close to his fingers. He blew it out, and

listened and lit another. It seemed to him that he could hear faint noises above. He lit another match, and went on ahead.

Someone—Ozzie Heid, probably—had thoughtfully left a flashlight looped with a piece of cord hanging from a nail at the foot of the stairs. It was old and battered and bound with black tape, and its beam was feeble. But it served. Nate passed through the large kitchen still faintly warm and faintly smelling of the last meal cooked, passed through several large pantries and anterooms. Massy old pieces of furniture filled with china and cutlery and linen and glass enough to serve, probably, the entire population of Nokomas at a sit-down supper, lined the walls. And ahead, at last, he recognized the huge double-doors which opened onto the great living room. He turned off the flashlight.

Faint light spilled out somewhere ahead. Nate waited for his eyes to adjust. It didn't take long. And so he came, finally, to the room where Joseph Bellamy lay, his grey face to the side, one palm pressing the rug, the other hidden from view somewhere beneath his chest.

There was no doubt in Nate's mind that the man was dead.

He looked around for the telephone. The room was in disorder. He saw the phone, but, before going for it, he quickly—as silently as he could—closed the door and turned both lock and night-latch. Then he picked up the phone and dialed 0. The thought occurred to him that he owed it to the man on the floor, his host and not-quite kinsman, to try artificial respiration. He knelt, taking the phone down with him; turned Bellamy on his back and looked once, quickly, into the intent and puzzled face. Then he pinched shut the cool flesh of the nostrils, covered the dry lips with his mouth, and breathed in. He released his fingers and listened to the whisper of the twice-used air, closed the escape and breathed in again.

He did this for some time, without observing the slightest effect.

And then he realized that the telephone signal had been droning on without once having been interrupted by the voice of the operator. He filled the lungs once more, but held the nostrils shut a second more than usual as, with his other hand he broke the telephone connection by pressing the stud; then he dialed 0 again. He resumed the mouth-breathing efforts. After a long while the buzz of the signal suddenly ceased. He grabbed for the phone and got hold of it just in time to hear the silence conclude and the signal's drone commence again.

Dizzy from his efforts, his pulse drumming heavily, he let the phone slip, slipped himself, and fell across the body. He heard a sound of surprise, too low to be an exclamation. A wild hope and excitement flew up in him, he glanced quickly at Bellamy's face . . . but it had begun to go loose and flaccid and it was more than ever the clay-gray face of a corpse . . .

There was no other sound he was aware of hearing, but he twisted his head around and up, so quickly it was painful, and he saw, standing in a doorway, a man who was perfectly strange to him: a young man perhaps a few years his senior, with a dark, outraged, astonished face.

For a few seconds they thrust stares at each other. Then, "I guard. I serve. I seek," said the other man. He seemed to say it unwillingly, dubiously and threateningly, somehow in the manner of a dog circling around and uncertain if it will be friend or foe.

Nate Gordon said, "What in the hell—"

The dark young man's face turned darker yet. He took a step forward, pointed a finger, stopped, clenched his fist, breathed noisily. Nate started to scramble up, the other man's head sunk, he crouched. Then, face twisting, he turned and ran back behind the door he stood in. His footsteps suddenly ceased. Nate ran after him. There was a thud. And there was no one in the room when Nate got there. No one in the room without windows, the room with no doors except the door he now stood in.

Someone else, perhaps, might have retreated—not necessarily out of cowardice, but out of helplessness. But Nate Gordon had not only read much cheap fiction, seen so many cheap movies and TV shows, he had himself written so much of it that he could no more stop doing what he now proceeded to do than he could have stopped breathing. He began to rap the paneled walls of this inner room from as high as he could reach right down to the floor. Nothing sounded hollow: this was not part of the script, the necessary, logically following sequence of *must*-events: but then almost at once something happened which was: Nate, stooping low and rapping near the floor, noticed a faint line of discoloration on the rug as it met the wall. Neither voice nor instinct that he could think of, but a vigorous imagination responding to the pressures of this new familiar situation, directed his next action.

He slid his fingers, knuckle-sides down, back along the rug . . . the tips of them did pass under the paneling . . . he levered and jerked . . . the paneling slid up . . .

The wall behind was solid.

Or—

Was it?

Perhaps the thing was just a trick of the lights, perhaps he was still dizzy, but— He came up closer to it and it seemed to quiver and recede, folding in upon itself in the manner of an optical illusion; and then it was gone. Beneath his feet Nate Gordon still felt the rug and the chill air of that windowless inner room in Darkglen House, but before and all around his face he saw—

But, did he *see?*

Once, before he had perfected his infallible sub-literary formula, Nate had written an article for an occult magazine on the subject of "eyeless sight," that singular but often-attested phenomenon "whereby the faculty of vision is situated elsewhere than in the retina of the eye." It did not come to him, therefore, as a complete surprise—merely as surprise enough to raise his short hairs and, seemingly, liquefy his heart—for him to realize he "saw" nothing while his eyes were open and that the moment he closed them he "saw" with what was apparently the entire epidermal surface of his face . . .

What he "saw" in that astonishing millisecond of a blink was too infinitely unfamiliar to register upon his unprepared mind. Shock. Blink. Shock. Blink. He screwed his eyes tight shut and turned his head, blazing with strange new vision, from side to side. And it was then he saw something immediately recognizable, but in its own way equally frightening: the stranger of only a moment ago, "staring" at *him* with the man's own eyes tight shut, and a short and ugly rifle in his hands. The weapon came up and out, Nate's mind said, quicker, probably, than it had ever said anything, *He can't sight that, so he'll fire from hand level*; and the thought was not complete when Nate saw again in his old sight the outer surface of the wall—and fell over backward from the sudden motion with which he had pulled in his head.

Aware, in some separate compartment of his confused mind that no bullet had followed him, wondering—in that same little mind-niche—if this was because nothing could pass through from *there* to *here* or if the rifle had not been fired after all, Nate righted himself and came forward on his hands and knees as if prepared to butt at the false wall (*all*

an illusion, someone assured him, calmly, in another mind-
niche; *not even a trick mirror, over-oxygenized or -nitro-
genized, rapture of the depths from breathing too much plus
the shock of breathing into a dead man's lungs: you'll come
to in a minute*) and thrust his head into and through it and
saw—

—saw the figure of his sudden and unknown enemy, vanishing backward as though falling down a vertical well, spinning
and dwindling and (here the well simile ceasing) darting off at angles and then—oh, small end of the telescope
indeed!—though shrunken, but still well within the range of
"vision," he seemingly turned to the right and ran upside
down at an angle of about eighteen degrees and vanished.

Nate stared a long while but there was no reappearance.
He withdrew his head. Whatever was there (wherever *there*
was!) was going to have to wait. Death, try at resuscitation,
something very close to attempted murder, and then . . .
That. A place which defied or ignored the laws of solids,
optics, gravity, and who knew what else. It was too much.
Too much for now. So Nate stayed on his knees a while,
and, while he was there, said a short prayer of little cohesion
but great intensity. Then he got up and pulled down the shell
of wooden wall which fitted the "wall" which was not. The
fit seemed as close as oil on water.

Back in the adjoining room again, he looked at the body
of Joseph Bellamy. Surely, any further attempts at mouth-
breathing would be more in the line of necrophilia than life-
saving. Suddenly Nate felt very sick and cold. He sat down
quickly in the deep, leathery chair and lowered his head. It
didn't make him feel very much better, but by and by he felt
well enough to try the telephone again. He had completed
dialing before he realized that it was Peggy Stone's number . . . and that it wasn't ringing. There was nothing in his
ear but the steady drone of an open—a supposedly open—telephone line.

So, once again he tried to get the operator. This time he
timed it by the old Seth Thomas clock on the wall: fifteen
minutes. No response. Then, methodically, he dialed every
number he could think of, including some from years back
which he knew were no longer occupied by those who once
had held them. If he could just reach somebody, anybody, he
could ask that body to call his/her local police with the
message. The . . . ah . . . message? *Mr. Joseph Bellamy
of Darkglen House was killed by an intruder who vanished*

into a wall, and to prove it I'll show you the wall he vanished into or rather through . . .

No. No, that wouldn't do. For one thing, he, Nate, didn't know, didn't know at all that the man he saw had killed Joseph Bellamy. It might be a good idea to see if there were any—Oh God!—life imitating cheap fiction again!—any signs of violence on the body. On the other hand, it might be a good idea to do nothing of the sort. Don't touch anything until the police arrive. Poor old lonely man there on the rug—already and for some time past, now: a thing. Very possible, though, he had just, well, died. Certainly he had looked unwell, unhealthy; certainly he had taken pills . . . well, tablets; capsules . . . Nate saw him. In fact, there were some right there, there on the table.

And still no reply from the buzzing telephone. Try to walk? To Nokomas? Twenty miles? In this weather? It might start snowing or storming before he even reached whatsitsname Corners. He didn't know and Ozzie hadn't said if anyone lived there now. No, no. Nothing to do but sit up with the dead until dawn, or whatever time the hired help arrived. He put the phone back on the table. From time to time he'd try it again. Meanwhile . . . He deliberated, rubbed his chin. He'd go and look for something to cover the body. And for something, Christ yes! something to drink.

"I was swept up by events," he said to himself later. And, "Oh, Gordon, you're a magnificent stylist and a great coiner of phrases as well."

Things seemed to arrange themselves around him, was what had happened. Keziah hadn't exactly screamed on see-ing the covered form on the floor when Nate, awakened by her knock, opened the door. She had given a loud gasp and put her red hands to her red face and then she began to talk and talk and *talk*—

"Oh, my Lord. Oh, my *Lord!* He's dead, it's happened, I knew it, I *knew* it. I knew it the minute I walked in the door this morning, I just felt it, 'Something ain't right,' I said to myself— *Glory! Ozzie!* Oh, were you here, were you *here?* Mr. Jordan? When it happened? *Ozzie! Ozzie! Glory!* Oh, what a shock it give me, here, let me sit down. Not that it's a surprise. Poor *man!* I'm going to start crying in a minute, thirty-five years I worked here for him, and before that, too, his uncle— Oh, it's no surprise. Here they come, I better go out and tell Glory, her nerves ain't—"

Her nerves weren't. It was quite a while before Ozzie and

Keziah—and, for that matter, Nate—could compose her suffi-
ciently for Ozzie to drive the both of them off. The phone still
would not respond and Glory refused, with signs of renewed
hysteria, to remain behind. "I can't help it, I can't *help* it!"
she declared, loudly, her nondescript face working. "You
know that, Oz. Ever since George was taken that time. You
leave me off at home, Emma'll have to quit work and stay
home with me today, I don't say it's right, he was a good
man, a good boss, but I can't help it I'll ask Sadie Snyder
can she come up and help you, Kezzy, but—*I*—can—*not.*"

So the old car started off, and not without difficulty. Keziah
from somewhere had produced a second glass. She seemed as
calm as Glory Smith had not. "Oh, there's so much to do. I
would hardly know where to begin. You said a prayer, didn't
you, Mr. Jordan? That's a good thing. Well, another one
won't hurt . . . Yes, she was right, he *was* a good man and
a good boss. He knew it was coming. We all knew it was
coming. First of all, we had *eyes*, didn't we? And then
besides he did tell us. 'Don't be frightened,' he said. 'Comes
to all of us,' he said. Said something I guess he read in a
book, not the Bible, though, but it was a kind of a nice thing
anyway. Said—'Joining the great company of the dead, for
they increase around us as we grow older.' I don't feel it just
yet, you know. Oh, I'll *feel* it by and by. Don't you worry.
It's too bad this had to happen to you, won't be much of a
vacation for you. Won't be for *me*, either, can tell you.
Remember when *old* Mr. Bellamy, oh dear, we were busy for
months—"

She broke off abruptly, finished the drop of brandy, got up
and padded over to the desk. "Here it is," she said, taking a
sheet of paper from the drawer. "Just where he showed me.
'Phone these people,' he said. 'See that they are informed at
once.' And— Mm-*hm*. Name with a line around it," she had
proceeded to dial a number while Nate sat watching, too
numb and tired to remind her that the phone was out of
order.

Only, it seemed, it wasn't.

"Mr. Ralph Wiedemyer, please," she said, reading. "Speaking? Over in Roman Hill, New York? Well, now, I've got a
sad duty to perform, Mr., and maybe you better sit down.
You knew Mr. Joseph Bellamy over in— Oh. Well, *yes*. Not a
surprise to you, either, I guess he— Well, we don't *know* yet,
Mr. Wiedemyer. But he had this bad heart in addition to
everything else and oh about eleven last night he rang this
buzzer in his room that connects with the guest cottage here

and Mr. Jordan, young man from— Jordan. That's right —
from New York, he was staying there and he come right over
but by the time he got here our poor dear Mr. Bellamy, he
had passed away . . .? Why, he had a *list*, that's how. Your
name was on it, you was to be called first. I guess I better
hang up now and call these other names. Yes. Yes. Well, I'll
give it to his lawyer and I guess *he* will call you again when
the arrangements have been all made. Not at all. Good-
bye. . . ."

So Nate just rode or coasted along with the story. He just
kept quiet about its nightmare elements, not being any too
sure about them, anyway. Not on this clear winter day with
the dull sun beginning its short climb up the bitter sky.
Keziah made the phone calls to attorney, bank, undertaker,
minister, and masonic lodge. "I'm going to go down and
make about five big pots of coffee and start some food going," she said, rising. "We'll need all of it. You, first, though.
All night long, poor Mr. Jordan, you'll get the first cup and
the very first plate. Only—" She paused at the door. "Maybe
you better turn off the electric heater. Don't know how soon
the undertaker can get here. Or how late."

Nate did. He heard her feet going down the hall. He
blinked sore-edged eyes. For the hundredth or the five-hundredth time, he looked at the blanket-covered body on the
floor. For the five-hundredth or perhaps only the hundredth
time he observed the rounded shape of one hip thrusting its
outline up. But this time the nagging thought surfaced: *The
way he's lying there he must be uncomfortable* . . . Ridiculous thought, but not ignoble. But now he understood it, he
had to act upon it, don't-touch-till-the-police-come or not. He
knelt on one knee, drew back the blanket from the lower
part of the body, winced a bit at sight of the thick white
ankle revealed as trouser leg rode up past sock, and tried to
make the minor adjustment. But the body did not adjust. He
rummaged and groped, found something . . . something
smooth and hard . . . pulled it out. The body settled
slightly and, covered again, no longer seemed to reproach
him.

He stared at what he saw.

The nightmare stirred again.

Keziah called.

Walking and holding it very carefully, Nate went over and
opened the door a bit, "Yes?" he asked.

"Mr. Jordan, I can't come up and be with you," she
called. "I've just got too much to *do*. I'm making a ham and

a leg of lamb and, oh, whatever I can find. I remember that when *old* Mr. Bellamy died there were just *dozens* of people here, even be*fore* the funeral, and they all got to be fed, it's not like the city here, you know, and, *well*, Mr. Jordan, but even if I can't stay up there *with* you—" She hesitated, then her voice plunged on, a bit quickly, "—you could come be down *here* . . . I suppose . . . If you like . . ."

He waited just a moment and then said, "Thank you, but I'll be okay up here." Her relieved tone told him that he had made the correct response, that Keziah, in thinking of him and his own possible feelings, had been thinking at least as much of that deeply felt and ancient customary law, *Thou shalt not leave the unburied dead to be alone.*

Closing the door again, Nate looked at what he held. A sort of pyramid of stone, though what kind of stone it was he could say or guess only that it appeared crystalline—using the term in its vaguest possible sense of color for which he had not quite a name, a tinge of pink, a touch of purple; it seemed to be changing shades in a subtle fashion while he was staring at it. But within the object, and running through it were lines and lines of glowing light. Sometimes they seemed to form a pattern, but this shifted and appeared to fracture with the faint pulse tremors of his hands. The lines were straight, they were curved, they moved at angles, they overlay one another, they were often infinitely close but indistinctly separate. And all this changed, changed, changed, yet did not ever entirely change; and always his eyes, attempting to follow, found themselves deceived.

Nate found himself certain of several things. For one, this thing was somehow connected to what lay behind that non-wall in the windowless room. For another, he was not going to tell anyone, *anyone,* about either one of them. Not now, at any rate. He felt an absolute conviction that it would be an act of idiocy, and of dangerous idiocy, to do so.

The form under the blanket had not of course grown smaller in the hours of lying there. Somehow, though, it seemed to have. Nate wrapped the stone and the bottle in his scarf and knotted them. He said, "Good-bye, Mr. Bellamy." He went into the adjoining room, slid up the wooden panel, walked backward through the wall, and slid down the panel. Then he closed his eyes.

The place he had come through appeared as a dark rectangle in a golden, glowing orifice of irregular shape at the end of a corridor. That was where the corridor went; clearly, then, it had to come from somewhere. Desiring to see how

the exit appeared from a different prospectus, he walked
backward and to the side, meanwhile turning his head a few
inches. He was not particularly surprised to see the dark
rectangle change in color, size, proportions, location—it was
no stranger than the effect of this new vision, so different in
kind and quality from ocular vision, so increased in area. He
compared the way the exit into Darkglen seemed to hop and
spin and move from side to side with everything else he was
seeing it do—he compared this with his memory of watching
the dark young man who had shot at him vanish. Evidently
it was the same phenomenon, viewed from two different
directions. He was moving . . . or the "door" was moving . . . or both were moving . . . or else, in some way,
neither was: but something else was happening.

Meanwhile, through the translucent sides of the corridor
he could see other ones. Some were parallel, others were at
different levels, or crossing his at different angles, or cutting it
through in wide parabolas—he passed through these with no
more than a flicker of awareness—or descending like shafts
from nowhere to nowhere; until, off in the distances, they
blurred and dwindled and were lost. A rather belated sense of
his own rashness now occurred to him. But all he did was try
to walk another few steps. It was not like walking on any
surface which he had ever trod before, but there was a
purchase for his feet, that was the main thing, and his feet
left the corridor—the "gate" through which he had come now
small but still visible and no longer changing—and he found
himself in a vast and vaulted area to one side of which he
saw a dark triangle.

He walked toward it, from time to time turning to reassure
himself that the way back was not vanishing, and, when he
got there, cautiously pushed an end of his scarf through it
and drew it back again. It seemed utterly unaffected. He
thrust through his head. He looked out upon a warm, wet,
narrow gully lined with great ferns. From somewhere above
and ahead came a deep, loud, and presumably animal grunting. Nate withdrew his head rather thoughtfully. "This is
quite a peep-show," he said. After rubbing his chin a while
he walked back the way he had come and left the open place
for the corridor. He intended to go back all the way, but
when he stepped through the rectangle once more he felt
sand yield beneath his feet, and, opening his eyes, saw a huge
red sun resting upon the horizon of an all-encompassing
desert.

His heart gave a great lurch of fear, his breath left him,

his lungs strained futilely for air, and his incredulous eyes observed a train or procession of what seemed to be unicorns winding across the dunes like a serpent. He stepped back, stumbled, fell on his knees in the darkness, found he could breath again, closed his eyes so as to be able to "see," and saw the two men. One of them had in his hand something rather like an automobile antenna with a hilt, ridiculous as this of course was; other than that the two men were identical: young, scantly and strangely dressed, hairy in some odd way which he could not quite put his finger on, and resembling no race or people which he had ever in his life seen or heard of. The one with the object thrust it at him. Nothing happened. The two spoke with each other, and their voices had a pleasant timbre, though seemingly puzzled. Nate was not frightened now.

And one reason why he was not was because he recognized the object as being identical with the one he had seen in the corner of the windowless room at Darkglen House.

Nate was a while with Et-dir-Mor before he remembered what was still wrapped up and knotted into his long woolen scarf. "Yes, yes, yes," the old man said, when he saw it. "A ward, a ward-stone. It is not precisely the same as mine, I suppose that no two are, as no two men are, not even my twin grandsons. But it is enough like mine . . . I will show it to you presently. Well. There can't be much doubt. Bel-am-My had the ward, he had the sword, he must have been a Watcher. I don't know them all. I couldn't. No one can. But there must be a group or guild or office or corps or caste . . . words! words!—who does know him. So this must go back to them."

They sat in a . . . Nate assumed he must call it, as he thought of it . . . in a room: a low-walled, furnished platform built up almost to second-story height within the great central chamber of Et-dir-Mor's three-tiered dwelling. An S-shaped table which, like a love seat joined and separated them, bore food and drink; and as Nate ate and drank he thought with some guilt of Keziah's promise that she would bring him the first cup of coffee and the first plate of food. Perhaps he ought not to have done as he did. There were a thousand good reasons for him not to have, but the curiosity which had been building up all night required more power to resist than he had had in his fatigued and light-headed condition. Of course they would wonder there at Darkglen what had become of him, but not for very long. There would be

just too much to do. Nate had no fear of their discovering
that the panel slid up: why should they? Besides, unless he
was completely mistaken, someone of those on the list Keziah called would have another on duty, so to speak, in jig-
time. *Duty*. Old Bellamy's conversation last night began to
make more sense now. A Watcher . . .

All alone there, year after year, a crystal gazer of a vastly
different kind, watching . . . watching . . .

"But what is it?" Nate asked. "What is it made of?"

Et-dir-Mor dropped his hand at the wrist in a gesture the
equivalent of a shrug. "We do not know. They may be pieces
of the Maze itself which split off from it, perhaps at the
moment of its creation. If it was created. Or perhaps later.
We have never heard of anyone actually finding one there.
The ones we know of have been among the Watchers forever, as it were, although there are many legends of them
having been stolen by or lost among those who didn't know
their use. Or who *did* know . . . or knew something . . .
and who would misuse it—if they could. I need hardly explain
to you—"

Hardly. That had been almost instinctively evident.

"It seems that there is something like cell memory at work
in these wards. That is, that if it is really a fragment of the
Maze, it shows something of the structure of the Maze. We
think so. That it adapts itself to show at any rate a certain
area of it, the area it is nearest to; and that, entirely out of
that area, it would change to mirror or to indicate another
one. Am-bir-Ros compared it once to a periscope. Another
time he said, 'It's like an immensely complex thermometer.
You have to learn to "read" it.' "

"Am-bir-Ros?"

"My friend, whom you may meet, who taught me English.
He comes from—not quite your time, I should guess; but
close to it. I don't know if he was before or will be after you.
Try some of this—"

His hand, with its curious, long, distinct white hairs offered
a container of something. Nate took it but did not take of it.
"Now, hold on . . . hold on . . . easy," he said. "You
mean that the, the Maze?—it doesn't just cross the dimensions
or whatever it is? It crosses *time* as well?"

The vessel, hourglass in shape, stayed suspended over the
table as they each held it with a hand, one hand on each
section of it. The gesture seemed mystical, hieratical. Then,
"Oh, yes, I mean that," said Et-dir-Mor. "Dimensions, times,
sections, sectors, parallels, places—all these and more, and

things for which we have neither name nor conception nor capacity. It was a fortuitous accident which brought you so easily from your place and time to ours. If, that is, if there be fortuity, if there are such things as accidents. But it *is*, I do assure you, it *is* a maze. So you were fortunate.

"You might quite easily have wandered in it until you died, you know. Oh, yes. Oh, yes. But do not be fearful. I am sure that you—at any rate, we can show you the way back. Some, we cannot. And some," he added, with a pleasant smile; "some, of course, do not wish to go back."

CHAPTER SEVEN

Some sort of private thing was clearly going on between the tall man and the short man. Some of it, probably, was endocrinal. The tall man swelled out at the middle—hip and thigh and rump and belly—and tapered at the ends: small head, hands, feet. The short man seemed momentarily about to undergo an explosion or implosion which would result in his being not short at all. For the moment (something about him seemed to say) he was holding himself in . . . but any moment now— There was something false and sly about the tall man, his good humors and his bad ones seemed alike assumed. The short man was all of a piece, but there was nothing reassuring in this; it was a piece of the same material that too many high school principals, boys' camp directors, and military and naval officers are made of: a texture or quality often dignified by the description, "ability to command"—the desire to bully, override, bear down—the capacity to do so by virtue of office—the habit of having done so for a long time and the confidence of continuing to do so for a long time.

There was another difference between them, for the tall man was the county sheriff and the short one was captain of the state police troop: dog's head and lion's tail. The sheriff appeared to be continually torn between the recollection that Nate had no vote in the county and the possibility that it wasn't impossible he someday might. The sheriff had only his one paid deputy beneath him and nobody above him except the sovereign citizen-voters—and, at least in theory, the governor of the state, who might (but probably wouldn't) remove him for misfeasance, malfeasance, and nonfeasance of office. He was a tradesman in his private life and a politician in his public one. Almost every legal paper he ever served and almost every arrest he ever made meant not only a fee earned and a duty done but an enemy made, a customer and a vote lost; he gave, therefore, the impression of a man busily engaged in trying to avoid being sucked up by his own rectal orifice. This was Sheriff Nobeldorf.

The public had no hold on Captain Congers; his eyes, when they turned from malefactors potential or kinetic, were directed toward a hierarchy he no longer entertained much hope of climbing. Middle age now held him fast, he hated the scene of his exile, found refuge from his bitter wife and severe superiors in the unshined boots of a trooper or the possibility of browbeating an offender against the general code.

Congers barked and snapped, Nobeldorf prowled and looked watchful. The immediate menace of the former seemed to hint, nevertheless, of possible and future protection based on experience; the present non-involvement of the latter threatened, just the same, future and possible menace growing out of ignorance and the need for popular reputation.

"I'd like a better explanation of where you have been!" Captain Congers bared his teeth.

"Oh . . . Just around," said Nate, vaguely.

Sheriff Nobeldorf arose and scratched his ass. "Maybe he took a nap," he suggested. "Must be a million beds in this house. Christ."

Nate wasn't sure if he was being offered an excuse to use or a trap to fall into . . . or if the tall man was merely thinking aloud.

A spasm of annoyance passed over the symmetrically seamed face of the state police officer. He ignored the sheriff, but not his remark. "We were all *through* this place. Went away and thought better of it and came back, I suppose. Well. What were you afraid of?"

Soft as lard, the sheriff asked, "Went where? Went how? Came back when?"

Nate said nothing. He was fully aware that he had not been arrested, not—in fact—accused of having done anything except causing his own absence and reappearance. This was not in itself a criminal offense and he was, he felt, not bound to explain it. He was also fully aware that these two men, individually or collectively, had the power of causing him much grief, and he desired not in the least to provoke them into remembering it (if, indeed, they needed any reminders) by any vocal declarations of what he felt he was not bound to do. So he continued to say nothing and tried to look vague rather than stubborn.

Meanwhile he went on mentally playing one questioner against the other. Congers had less to gain by involving Nate in any criminal charge than Nobeldorf had. He didn't have to seek re-election, a conviction would mean less to him. On the other hand, he had less to lose: an acquittal would mean equally less to him. He didn't have to consider the cost to the local taxpayers of a trial whose expense was unjustified by the satisfaction of a sentence.

"How soon'll they have that report, you suppose?" Nobeldorf asked.

Congers looked at his watch, shrugged irritably. "*Report* . . ." The word echoed, silently loud. Report . . . report . . . what kind of a report? Only one answer supplied itself: a medical report. It fit in. Fit in with the fact that he had been neither charged nor accused, fit in with earlier questions concerning his relationship to Joseph Bellamy and did he know the contents of Mr. Bellamy's will. Yes, indeed. Also: no, indeed. Suppose—damned unlikely to Nate—that he was the dead man's heir?—maybe a lot less unlikely to Congers and Nobeldorf. After all, he had been invited to Darkglen, he was related by marriage. Suppose the report were to show that neither the bad heart nor anything else of the sort had caused death. Suppose . . . after all, Ned hadn't examined the body, hadn't turned it over . . . a bullet hole? A knife wound? No . . . No one had searched Nate or even asked if he owned gun or knife. So . . . well . . . a contusion, say. Something like that. "Deceased met his death by violence and Accused stood to profit by his death." They didn't talk like that in the United States, but, still.

On the other hand. If Bellamy's death was from purely natural causes, then Nate's presence was fortuitous, his absence of equally no significance. More: if Bellamy had died a natural death *and* Nate were his heir, *well* . . . Nobeldorf, at any rate, would assuredly not want the local rich man (for all he knew) to have cause to remember him for ill.

If the report was okay, then everything was okay. And if it weren't, what then? "*I saw another man and he walked through that wall inside* . . ." Not at all the trite situation of not being believed; it was of comparatively little importance if he were believed or not—concerning the other man, that is. He had only to show them the Maze in order for them to believe in the Maze.

Which was to say, he had only to show them the Maze in order for them to make use of the Maze.

Them—and millions of other *Thems.*

The telephone rang.

"It's working now," Nate said. Congers and Nobeldorf looked at him as the former picked up the phone, but nothing was said except the former's curt, "Hello!"

"No . . ." he said, after a moment. "No . . . No . . . I don't know." His sigh was exceedingly brief and he hung up.

Nate said, "I'd like to make a phone call."

Sheriff and captain exchanged looks. "I don't see why not," the sheriff murmured. Congers's grunt, as he handed Nate the instrument, seemed to indicate that he didn't see why not, either, but wished he did.

Peggy's response to the single ring was so swift that she must have been waiting for it, next to it. And she had evidently (a) been waiting for it a long time and (b) spent all of that time thinking of what she was going to say. It took her quite a while to say it, with Nate making the traditional brief and futile interjections of the straight man in a situation comedy: stupid old Dad, as it might be. Boiled down and strained twice, it amounted to the fact that PO-LICE had come to the office where Peggy worked (WORKED: she didn't OWN the place) and had questioned her about Nate. She had worked in that place for seven years and hoped to go on working there for another seven years and in all that time (her remarks now seeming to include the future as well as the past) the police had NEVER come and asked about ANYONE. How did it LOOK? Had Nate any idea what a thing like that could do to a person's REPUTA-TION? And not only the POLICE! EVERYONE had asked her about it, after the police left. COHALLAN had asked her. CHANDOS had asked her. RUTHERFORD and WEINSTOCK and MERRY-ELLEN and even that low, slimy, son-of-a-bitch, DONAHO! had asked her. DONAHO! whose attitude notoriously was, If it smells bad, by all means throw it into the fan!

Nate said *But.* He said *I.* He said *Listen.* He said *Peg.*

That was bad enough. That was quite bad enough. But what hurt, what really hurt, was that the police said that they'd found her name and phone number in Nate's suitcase. How could anyone be so stupid? How could anyone be so

careless? How could anyone be so absolutely and utterly
in—dif—ferent? to someone else's welfare? as to leave her
name and phone number in his suitcase? This passed Peggy's
capacity to understand. She did not, did not, did not understand how he could have done it.

Nate said *Oh for.*

Peggy said that she had only one question to ask. She
would like, she would really like a reply to it. She was asking
it civilly, she was asking it calmly, she was asking it politely;
making no reproaches, no references whatsoever to the fact
that her name had probably been ruined forever and her
career and professional reputation had suffered a stigma
which would certainly never wear off; no: none of that. Not
a word, not a word, not a single word. She wasn't even
angry. Just curious. Would Nate mind answering that question? He really wouldn't? He was sure? Good.

"How could you do it?"

Her voice echoed in his ears long, long after he had hung
up without answering. He saw the mouths of Sheriff Nobeldorf and Captain Congers moving, but if they said anything,
he didn't hear it. He saw Keziah come in with plenty of the
food and coffee she had spoken of—when was it? He wasn't
sure. He wasn't even approximately uncertain today, probably, earlier today—and she looked at him with reproach—
and with no more than a measure of kindly curiosity as she
(it seemed) urged him to eat and drink. Obediently he
moved to the table, cut, poured, stirred, swallowed.

I have seen the sun rise at midnight.

The famous phrase, where was it from? Lucius Apuleius,
probably; *The Golden Ass*; but it was a symbolic reference,
not to any Arctic dawn, but to the still-mysterious drama of
the Eleusinian Mysteries. Nate had seen something more
unsettling than that, greater wonder than if he had seen,
literally and actually, his own sun rise in his own midnight.
The thought of it was like a blow to him, delayed shock or
arrested wonder. Circling around it, striking its own blows
whenever the opportunity offered, was the smaller (but not
small) shock of Peggy. So Nate sat there, stonefaced, making motions, like a man dancing on the crust of the pit: let
him dance lightly, dance delicately.

"What?"

This time Nobeldorf had answered the phone, was waving
him to come answer it.

"Who?"

"I said, 'Mr. Wiedemyer.' This is I don't know oh maybe

the fourth, fifth time he's been calling," the sheriff said, covering the mouthpiece with the cushion of his hand. "Well, I guess he must have a, sure, legitimate concern, he was on Mr. Bellamy's list; anyway, he's on the phone—" He raised it to his mouth, smiled a bland and automatic and sebaceous smile—"Here's Mr. Gordon now, Mr. Wiedemyer."

Nate's eye, as his hand took the phone, rested on the opposite wall, on a sepia photograph framed in dark wood— this house in the days of its greatness and glory . . . whatever the hell such words meant, applied anywhere, let alone here . . . His mouth made some sort of acknowledgment.

Polite, fussy, tired, precise, excited, unhappy, cautious was the voice or the molecular reproduction of the voice in his ear. "—a rather nice or rather nasty little monopoly the legal profession enjoys in that state. I realize it is not your fault, sir; I am, believe me, although I cannot explain now, trying to help you as much as," the shortest of pauses, "myself. It seems that being admitted to general legal practice in that state is not sufficient, it is also necessary to be admitted to practice in each individual county. That county's bar association consists of exactly six members. Mr. Johnstone, Mr. McDaniel, and Mr. Brandon do not take trial work—their phrase in each case: 'I don't take trial work.' Mrs. Arendts is in bed, sick. Mr. Sweet is out of town. That leaves Mr. Morton.

"I believe I have made exactly fifteen phone calls to Mr. Morton. He assures me there is no cause for alarm. Nothing will take place in the county, forensically speaking, without him being aware of it before it can be finished. He may or may not take the case—if there turns out to be a case—if he has time—if he receives the retainer which I have wired— Have I been too pre-occupied with my own grievances? Are you in immediate difficulties? Or is your position merely equivocal? The wire may be tapped, you know," he added, calmly.

"The position is as stated," Nate said, carefully. Tapped by whom? he wanted to ask. And not caring what the answer was. "Thanks for your interest," he said.

Mr. Wiedemyer actually said something which sounded very much as though it were *tut-tut*. "Here is the most important thing. Listen quite carefully. I cannot go to see you. I am trying to find someone . . . someone whom I will know personally . . . who will be able to go there to see you. *And on general and other specific principles*. I wonder if you understand what I—"

Responding to who knows what fugitive impulse, Nate said, "It's like trying to see with your eyes shut."

There was, for this conversation, a fairly long pause. Then Mr. Wiedemyer said, "The important thing is: if you have it, don't surrender it. And do not trust, do not follow strangers. *Timor Danaos et dona ferentes.* None may appear. Someone else is currently trying to get to where you are. I repeat, and I warn: Do not trust! And now I must discontinue this conversation. There's so much to do, there are too few of us, you must know the infinite importance—"

"I do. I'll remember. Good-bye."

He turned to see that meanwhile several strangers had entered the room. One of them at first struck his eye as being familiar—a sallow, stiff-looking man with clipped, gray hair. The other was evidently familiar at least to both Congers and Nobeldorf, with whom he immediately entered into casual, bluff conversation; a large, red-nosed and self-confident man. They addressed him as "Jack."

"Well, Jack, hey—"

"Oh, hello, Jack, have you—"

He, Nate, couldn't hear the end of the question because the third man was speaking to him, Nate.

"Mr. Gordon, Mr. Jamieson Swift has engaged us to look out for you in this matter, and we have engaged Mr. John Morton, who is a member of the local bar. By 'we,' Mr. Gordon, I mean the firm of which I am a member—Mathesson, Peabody, Farrel, and Smith—my name is Thomas Farrel Smith." He gave Nate a firm but not unpleasantly firm handshake. Thomas Farrel Smith was a small, slight man with pale, smooth skin and dark, smooth hair. His smile and the glance it contained seemed to say that he was pleasantly impressed with Nate.

Nate was mildly surprised, at least he thought he was, and a bit more than mildly pleased. The man with the red nose was discussing a bear hunt with Nobeldorf and Congers. The gray-haired man did not, at second look, seem a bit familiar. Nate said, "Such dispatch doesn't seem typical of Jamie. Not that I'm—"

Smith said, with a rueful smile, "Not that I'm, either, but— Well, it's been on the radio and the television and in at least some of the newspapers. To tell you the truth, we actually represent Mr. Swift in connection with other business matters. And it was we who called this to his attention. He was naturally upset and immediately asked us to do what we could." His voice dropped in tone and he said, with a glance to the side, "Here you can watch what is called, for some curious reason, 'the democratic process in action.' I assure you, it is a much more interesting show than either radio or television . . ."

Morton, having wound up the bear hunt, turned to Nate and he said, "Well, young fellow, are these two yokels giving you a hard time?"

"Now, Jack—"

"Ah, come on, Jack—"

But Morton waved them aside. "You're poor old Joe's nephew by marriage, aren't you?" he asked. He walked over, shook his hand, patted him on the back. "Too bad that this had to turn out like this, first time he had a chance to see you in years. Well, naturally . . . Both in the army, your brother and you, dead men, seeing dead men, no novelty. But . . . you know . . . funny thing—nothing to laugh at, not what I mean—odd—seems *different*, somehow, quiet, decent, civilized place like this. Old man asks you to come up and stay with him—nearest kin he has—dying. We all knew it. You didn't. Quite a shock. Stayed with him, though, faithfully, all night, all morning, didn't move from his side, covered him up decently, Kezzie told us, yes, yes."

He sighed, nodded. "All flesh is as grass," his sigh said. "The vanity of human wishes," his sigh said, "He who believeth in me shall not die," he nodded. "You went for a walk to be alone for awhile when you saw the whole goddamn cavalcade coming down the drive like Coxey's Army—Mat, when in the *hell* is the State going to get you a new car, the one out there is a dis*grace*, for Christ's sake, there's only one thing to do: you got, how many troopers? *you* know how many troopers. Plus your wife. Plus me. Plus *my* wife. My son. My daughter. My son-in-law. Okay. The only thing to do is we catch Oscar Hamilton and pin his ass to the mat. I mean, he's not in the General Assembly in response to some law of *nat*ure, for Christ's sake. He only won the nomination by exactly thirty-seven votes, you know? All *right*. Tomorrow night's his night at the firehouse, and if he votes down 't the Statehouse the way he plays poker down 't the firehouse, then: Oyez, oyez, and may God save this honorable Commonwealth, is all I got to say.

"Elmer Nobeldorf isn't in any too better of a shape either, now I come to think of it," said John Morton (Esquire), rubbing his red, red nose and gesturing with fluttering eyebrows at a cut-glass decanter on the sideboard. "Ah, thanks, El; old Joe knew how to buy booze, poor Joe. Have one, El.

It's therapeutic, you owe it to the citizens, protect your
health. Drop dead from the cold and frost, bottoms up,
here's hair on your balls, you won't have to worry about
Clyde Benchley, he, what'd he do? lost out by two-twenty-
two first time he run in the primary; only ninety-*one*, this last
time, Tsk," Jack Morton shook his cocked head. "Clyde
*Bench*ley as sheriff! Well, lots of people seem to like him, he
was sucking up to *me*, believe it or not, only last week. Well,
well, young fellow, you behaved altogether admirably on this
occasion; Mat Congers and El Nobeldorf obliged only in
their official capacities; sure you'll all be great friends: well.
    "What's he charged with?" he asked.
    "He isn't exactly *charged*—"
    "We're waiting for the re*port*—"
Morton's expression was that of an archbishop who has
seen his choirboys tumble out before the altar mother-naked.
"Not. *Charged*?" he cried, astonished, almost speechless. Almost. "You mean, he has *not* been taken before a magistrate? He is being *detained* here? You-know-better-than-that.
Not even arrested! Well, boys, one thing you've done. Not
only we don't need to bother with that writ of habeas corpus
Judge Fleming is waiting in his office to sign if it becomes
necessary, but you've—I *hope*—I could be *wrong*—I *believe*
you've saved yourselves from a suit for false arrest, which
otherwise this young man, he may for all we know be the
new and rightful owner of the very floor we stand on—
    "Button your coat up, Mr. Gordon. Let's go. After *you*."
He shook his head, jowls flapping reproachfully, at the two
peace officers.
    "Now, Jack, don't be—"
    "Listen Jack, I only—"
But their hearts didn't seem to be in it.
    Attorney Smith, his fine, dark brows arched quizzically,
bowed slightly and gestured slightly, toward the door. Nate
said, "I'll be right with you . . . 'Even kings must live by
nature,' " he added. He went through the other door, rapidly,
entered the small, cold, quiet water-closet, flushed the close-
stool. While it roared and gurgled, he, even more rapidly,
went to the end of the corridor and opened the window. He
strode quickly to the other end and opened the door there.
Then he returned to the room where Joseph Bellamy no
longer lay on the floor. He paused a moment and pressed his
wood against the door frame. A wave of cold and near-
nausea swept over him. He swallowed, hard.
    There wasn't any doubt in his mind, finally, why the sal-

low man with the clipped gray hair had looked familiar. Man never identified, man never introduced. Ralph Wiedemyer's warning. *Timor Danaos et dona ferentes.* Beware the Greeks when they come bearing gifts. This man might have been father, uncle, cousin—but kin, kin, close of kin—to the dark young man whose appearance, challenge, threat, had occurred so soon after Bellamy's last alarm and death.

Nate Gordon entered the inner room, closed the door, pulled up the wall, stepped through, pulled it down behind him.

He took five or six uncertain steps and then, watched—blinking, blind, light, darkness, spinning, whirling, roaring, blackness, whiteness, sickness, shadow, sharpness, dimness, glory, horror, silence, stillness, rest.

Afterward, though how long or how far afterward he knew not and no search could make him know for not even the event would teach him in its hour, he walked down a long cube tube of the richest golden crystal—measured pace with infinite grace and dignity, upon the tips of his toes and the balls of his feet, to the accompaniment of music of sakers, serpents, spinets, tambours and triangles. His walk was a dance, a sacred, hallowed, hallowing, holy dance. He came out into the Temple of En-lil, the Hei-gal of the Lu-gal, and his dance was a walk, a sanctifying, fructifying, pollinating walk.

He took the waiting priestess by her narrow, painted waist and possessed her and begat a godling upon her, and he arose and departed and affirmed to the few who dared to lift adoring, glazed, and glowing eyes, eyes like almonds, arrows, and like kohl; affirmed to them with gestures and the very gait of his walk, dance, dance, walk, dance, that neither U-perath nor Hid-dek-el would allow a drop too few nor suffer one too much, but both would water the valleys and trees and fields so that the steps of the ziqquratu would flow with myrrh, with honey, with butter, and with cream.

Afterward he departed, in search of Et-dir-Mor. This had not been his land after all. But it had been perhaps worth his while to have made the error.

He fled down a funnel through which blew ice and snow and rime and powdered hail and came out in a gust upon a plain where naked men whose shoulders and feet alone were wrapped in crackling hides thrust their fingers into huge and faintly steaming dung-masses and besought him with words, with gestures, and with mimings to tell them which way through the storm the great red mammoths had fled not long before, not long before at all. But he would not as he could not and strode back upon the blast the way he had come, back up and back down the funnel.

He sat and mused a long while at a point where seven cities glowed at the arm-ends of seven branch roads, each different as day from white, and watched them turn and revolve like the points of a great, slow Catherine wheel as he walked down the hub to the under sea grot where the mermen come to woo each other when their women have gone ashore to kindle and to bear. Their kink green beards adrifting and afloat in the gentle-currents, they gestured at him with their six soft arms and rolled their glaucous eyes. "Where is the Gate which leads to the land of Et-dir-Mor?" he asked them. Bubbles like streams of pearls rose from under their feet.

"Your story is a fantasy," the Stated Sages told him, fingering their lip furrows. "Your speech is a fantasy, and your clothes are fantasies as well, as well, as well." They nodded, but their manner was friendly. "Striving only for reality inevitably results only in fantasy, and to prove it, to prove it, to prove it, here is a fellow sickling. He also suffers from fantasy, as you may see from the fact that he wears the same clothes and speaks the same speech. He may or may not, depending on his immediate condition, incline to tell you his story, his story, his story; but we assure you it is exactly the same."

The dark young man in the red hunting shirt cleared his throat. "Look, that was a mistake on my part, getting mad and behaving like that that time the other night," he said. "I'm sorry."

Nate said, "What happened to Mr. Bellamy?"

The man scowled, shrugged. "He got in my way and I shoved him. I mean, I just *shoved* him. It wasn't my fault. Listen," he said, essaying a crooked grin, "we better stick together. Okay? I can show you a way out—besides the one you came in by, I mean."

Nate considered. "Okay," he said, after a moment. They walked off together through the great black stone.

The Stated Sages nodded at one another. "Now they have fantasied that they have no substance," they said. They rubbed their lip furrows and they sighed. Then they turned themselves inside out and went down the ramp for a sand bath.

"You first, now," said the red shirt.

"The Hell you say. That was a firearm you pointed at me."

"I said I was *sorry*, didn't I?"

"Don't follow strangers," Wiedemyer said. But did it make sense to let strangers follow *you*? when they had only very recently tried to kill you? Answer: No.

"Tell you what," Nate said; "we'll go side by side. Okay? Okay."

"Let's shake on it," said the other, and then tried to throw Nate over his back. There was quite a tussle, but Nate—by dint of beating his opponent to several dirty tactics—won. That is, he floored his man, and when the latter lunged at his leg, he side-stepped and kicked him smartly a few times in the side of the head. The man stayed down. He had a revolver in his pocket. Nate thumped him on the skull with it for good measure. Then he took off the fellow's shoes and tied his hands behind his back with his own socks.

" 'Fare thee well, my own true love,' " Nate sang; "*tum-tee-tum-tee-tah. Tum-tee-tum-tee-tum—tee-tum—little b'ar' feet on the floor . . .' "

By now he was no longer quite sure of where he was, but it certainly made no sense to remain there. He proceeded onward. Once or twice he had a nasty fright, as for instance the time he saw the body lying half-in and half-out of an opacity which indicated the presence of a gate. It was unclothed and chitinous and part of a spurred foot fell off as he nudged it with his shoe. He thought that he would not investigate what lay on the other side of the opacity. He did wonder, though, on the nature of the world the creature had come from.

It was almost immediately afterward that he heard the whistling sounds, like guinea pigs at first, then, as they grew nearer, too loud to be that. He saw only three of them at first, then the smaller one a moment later, all gamboling and tittuping and butting each other now and then. The first sight was the shocking one—three of them to his one: and they quite strange of form; or, if not quite that strange, then familiar-seeming chiefly by resemblance far from reassuring. And, in that place or in any place of that nature, almost hideously proper and peculiar to it. But there was something too innocent in their manner for fright to be maintained. So he stayed where he was and watched as they approached. After all, where was he to flee? Into that last portal where the exoskeletonic thing lay?—death-world that it probably was.

So he stayed put, but kept his hand on the revolver in his pocket.

And then they saw him. For a moment they ceased their romping and whistling. But for a moment only; then they came on. Their blocky bodies were rather man-like, though two of them were clearly female, and they were tridigital. But it was none of this, nor the symmetric wartiness of their skins, which immediately arrested attention. It was their heads, like great, rounded wedges, which caught both the eyes and the imagination. The flaps of integument, like ears. The bossy protuberances, like great, elongated warts. Or . . . like horns.

Minotaurs!

Up they came, frisking and gamboling once more, in a manner suggesting a game of follow-the-leader. Then, almost at his side, they turned away and began what may not have been, but which seemed to be hardly anything other than, a game of tag with the cub or calf. So benign was their manner, indeed, that it was almost absent-mindedly that he reached out and patted the proferred head of the "bull" as he watched the curious antics of the child. For some time they sported around about him; then, with more whistles and wavings and prancings, they were off. He turned and watched them until they vanished from sight.

This time Darius Chauncey was on duty. The fact, however, seemed to give him only a minimum of pleasure. "Thunderation," he said, letting his "sword" fall to his side, and switching it lightly against his bare, bronzed legs. "*You* ain't no Chulpex."

"No," said Nate. "I guess not."

The Watcher sighed disgustedly, shook his head. "Too much sugar for a penny. Wasted my time, trackin' you down, comrade." He pronounced it, *cum-raid*. He stood up on his toes and stretched. "Well, I wunt waste no more. Git back now, soon's I kin, take up where I left off with them gals with the big bubs an' the flouncy skirts." He grinned, winked, started to turn away.

"Hey, hold on. That sounds interesting."

Chauncey stared him down. "Yes, I bet it does. But don't let it git to soundin' *too* interestin'. Becuz you ain't a-goin' through. *I* am the top bully in that there manger, cum-raid, an' I aim to keep it thataway. You go on along, now, an' find your own pretty-place. Nothin' personal, now, but the decision is firm—not subject to review by any other try-bew-nal. Not while my name's Darius Chauncey."

Nate eyed him speculatively, decided to postpone any attempt at violence as long as possible. "I'm heading for Red Fish Land. You ever heard of it, Mr. Chauncey?"

He nodded, rubbed his chin. "Have, some. This ain't it. This is *Crete,* that's what it is. Ancient Crete—though whether ante- or post-diluvian, cain't say, never havin' been much inclined to religion of a muchness." A reminiscent look came over his face. "Got no objections to the local church, though. No, in-deed. Takin' up sarpints ain't the only thing them sistren do real well, I kin tell you. But I better not tell you too much. Mind what I say now: Just you keep on down the pike and find you some pretty-place of your own, you don't like it where you come from . . . Guess you don't come from very far or different than I did. Say. You got anything to smoke?"

Nate was about to shake his head, remembered that the phrase was an archaic idiom referring to a cigar, patted his breast pocket. It was still there—Joseph Bellamy's after-dinner gift. He held it up, drew it back.

"Rassle you for it, if you like. Or—"

"Just show me how to go to where I'm going, that's all."

"Red Fish Land. Hmm . . . Okay. I dassn't get too far from home base. I'll take you's far I kin, then draw you a kind of map for the rest. Deal, cum-raid?"

It was a deal. Darius Chauncey had gone back to his own little one-man colony in Minoan Crete to savor his prime brown Havana ("After I've knocked me off a nice lee-tle piece, cum-raid.") and Nate was following his map. It involved leaving the Maze and crossing a dreary stretch of moor or heath, wet and cold and lowering. It had the advantage of being—so Chauncey said ("My word on it as a Union officer, cum-raid.")—both short and easy to find, as well as devoid of danger. It was the sort of place one might expect to find at least three weird sisters, poking up the fire and complaining that the liver of the last Jew had been insufficiently blasphemied. He didn't find any, but he did not at all expect to find what he did, viz. Mr. Jackson.

Nate was able to entertain his mind with wandering thoughts, such as the weird sisters, instead of looking for, say, the third blasted oak on the left past the fork in the road; because there was no oak as well as no road, and, hence, no fork. He emerged out of the side of a low hill and headed straight down the very slight grade of the land toward the pond. This pond, Chauncey had assured him, was the only marker needed. He had gone perhaps half way when he heard a voice calling behind him.

He spun around, hand on the revolver, thinking that perhaps its owner had somehow got unraveled and was exercising the right of hot pursuit as well as that of hue and cry.

What he saw was someone strange to him, dressed all in black, and hurrying toward him over the heath, waving his hands in a manner which seemed, somehow, indefinably, strange. As, however, the man was waving both hands and had nothing in either; was walking and not running, Nate decided to relax . . . in a wary sort of way. He kept his fingers on his weapon, though, resolved to clench and aim through the cloth the first time the hands stopped waving and dipped into *their* pockets—if the garments had pockets to dip into, that is. They were rather odd garments, but not exceedingly odd . . . coat . . . trousers . . . Just a bit puzzling as to cut and drape and style.

Inspired by an antic humor, Nate said, when the man was close enough, "Dr. Livingston, I presume?"

"What? No, no. Not a physician or otherwise designated by title. Name is Jackson." The hands floundered a bit, uncertainly, finally deciding on offering the right one. Nate took it. The grip was strong, though on the clammy side. Nate reflected on the anomalies of this. Popular fiction held the handclasp to be an important indication of character. A strong grip reflected a strong personality: upright, it went without saying; and a soft grip reflected a soft, or weak, or morally inferior character. Sly, probably. And a clammy grip was the very worst of all. In popular fiction, though, "soft" and "clammy" always went together—hand in hand, as it were. Nothing was said anywhere about *strong*, clammy grips. Puzzling. Puzzling.

"We have common goals," said Mr. Jackson.

"How sociological."

The quip, gratuitous, passed over Jackson's head. Oyster-eyed, he looked at Nate. "Red Fish Land and your home. First the first, then the second. Common goals, common cause. Agreed?"

The air was wet and cold and dim. Nate looked at Jackson, and the words, "Rum cove," came into his mind. He shrugged. No one could have looked more normal than the young man in the red hunting shirt.

"You tend to simplify things, Jackson," he said. He wondered, mildly, where this place was. It might have been an as-yet-unoccupied Hell or Tantalus designed for real estate "developers"—miles and miles of empty land, and not a bulldozer in the house. "Maybe you oversimplify them. Like, who in the Hell are you and what in the Hell do you want with Red Fish Land? And, like, what makes you think I'm in such a rush to get back home just right now? Hey?"

Mr. Jackson's face seemed not at all disturbed by these questions. His hands flip-flopped a bit more, fell finally into a gesture toward the pond ahead.

"That appears to be water," he said. "It is not. It is a Gate. Your troubles appear to be insoluble. They are not, nor your questions unanswerable. Red Fish Land. There is someone there who has no proper right to be there. He must be found. There is a woman at home who has no proper right to be angry, though she is. And there are those who suspect you of great error, though you are innocent. To say nothing of those who have pursued you—not this one. Not Jackson. Not me."

Nate looked at him, made a wry mouth, rubbed it. "The fact that you know the questions," he said, a mite grudgingly, "tends to make me think you might really know the answers. What are you, really? A sort of walking delegate for the Watchers' Union."

Jackson straightened himself. He was on the tall side. "Your suggestion may not be altogether wrong," he said. "Well. There is the Gate. Mutual aid, mutual objectives?"

Nate shivered in the raw, wet air. Even the weird sisters, he reflected, at least had a fire and something hot to drink.

"Macduff or not," he said. "Lead on."

CHAPTER EIGHT

They left the drear and empty moor behind them and walked on into the pond as confidently as the Children of Israel had walked into the Red Sea. The waters did not divide this time, though: they seemed to recede, to fold in . . . to vanish . . .

And there again was the darkness which vanished paradoxically and abruptly as they closed their eyes, and there, in

the odd, extensive, and paroptic vision which it gave as its
gift were the burning golden corridors of the Maze.

They turned right, they turned left, they turned up, down,
aside and doubled back along a parallel lane. They passed
through an outside, through a screaming, thronging carnival
of masks and merriment. The way out here (which was also
the way in there) was not as it was supposed to be: seemingly the ground level, where they sought, had sunk. Nate
held Jackson on his shoulders—he was lighter, though older
and taller—and Jackson groped and felt and finally found it;
he scrambled in and reached down and helped Nate get up
and in.

"It might be easier," Nate said, after his eyes had once or
twice forgetfully opened and he had stumbled, sightless, over
his own feet; "it might be easier to get a pair of opaque
glasses." Jackson just grunted. Nate sang,

> " 'They rode on and they rode on,
> They rode by the light o' the Moon.
> Until they cam' to the bonnie burn's side,
> And there they hae lichted doun . . .' "

What they came to, actually and eventually, was a pocket
filled with sound and spray. "Must we go through that?"
Jackson inquired. He turned his head from side to side,
flagged his hands.

"Seems like it," Nate said. "Cover your nose and mouth
with your hands . . . Follow me, men! I'm right behind
you!"

The torrent thundered down upon them, struck and blud-
geoned and buffeted its blows upon them. Only for a moment,
though—then the waterfall lay behind them and they saw,
through eyes smarting a bit from water, a land of rounded
hills and rounded trees. In the distance, a line of tall machines moved diagonally through the cultivated fields.

"I suppose it figures," Nate said, slowly, stripping the
water off face and hair with his fingers and the edge of his
hand, "that Red Fish Land would have more than one doorway into it via the Maze. Are we far from Et-dir-Mor's
territory, do you know?"

Jackson said that they were not very far. Nate turned
away as Jackson continued talking, saying that they could
not go immediately to Et-dir-Mor, had to take care of the
other matter first: his, Jackson's, personal quest or business.
Nate heard what he was saying, but he was staring away

from the sun and opening and shutting his eyes. A curious thing had just happened. It had seemed to him that part of Jackson's head had gone translucent and that there were odd-looking things partly visible inside of it. This was probably a left-over from the paroptic vision of the Maze; could, in fact, be only that . . . sort of the thing that sometimes remains on the retina after the eyes close, in normal vision. Of course Nate could not explain it in terms of either normal or paroptic vision. He knew, after all, nothing about the latter except his personal experiences with it.

And when at last satisfied that his eyes had now come round all right, he turned back toward Jackson (who had ceased speaking), he saw that Jackson, too, had turned away and had his hands to his own face. "Don't be alarmed," Nate said. "The same thing just happened to me—" and he explained it as best he could.

"That is probably what it was," the other agreed. His face looked now perfectly normal . . . or at least as near to perfectly normal as it ever had. For, cook him sweet or cook him sour, Jackson remained basically a "rum cove." However . . .

"Sort of funny smell in the air here," had you noticed, Nate asked. "Sort of . . . damp, raw earth; something like that? I didn't notice it the last time I was here . . . Did you?"

Jackson hesitated. Then he made one of his odd, uncertain gestures toward the machines moving through the distant fields. "It is because they are stirring up the earth over there," he said. The wind didn't seem to be coming from that direction, but there seemed to be no other explanation, and besides, the matter was of less than microscopic importance. Also, he had something else on his mind.

"Should we strip down and wait for our clothes to dry in the sun?" he asked.

Jackson's reply to this was immediate. He thought it very unwise, there was likelihood the weather (uncertain, hereabouts) would change suddenly, there were insects, this, that, the other thing. Nate suddenly grew tired of the matter. "Okay, okay, we'll do it the old army way and let the damned clothes dry on us. It might be quicker that way—heat from inside as well as from out. But, *I* am going to take off my *shoes*—" he bent, grunting, then sat down, tugged. "If there's one sound above another I can do without, it's that damned squilch—squilch—squilch—"

But the sound continued to accompany their progress

along the soft turf; Jackson, evidently, preferred to keep his shoes on.

It couldn't be said that Jackson, shoes on, attracted more attention than Gordon, shoes off, from the few people whom they met. Curious, however, though the habitants clearly were, they remained true to the level of decent courtesy which Nate continued to think characteristic of the country. And he winced to think what would happen were any of them, in their own costume and with their distinct and different physical appearance, to show up in his own country—the mocking yahoos, the beggarly and bothersome brats of children, the quarter-wits shouting unsolicited "pleasantries" from passing cars. The whole nasty syndrome of what can happen and generally does to anyone who presumes to take literally the assumption of "It's a free country," who dares raise the dread, unarguable challenge of, "How come you have to be different?"

What Jackson might be saying to them, Nate couldn't tell for sure. Indeed, the fellow seemed to speak to them so low that Nate could barely hear him, let alone comprehend him. His voice was flatter, harsher, even though almost imperceptible. The Old Man, the Small Boy, the Good Wife—Nate, not knowing their names, thought of them as types—the Maiden Fair, the few others whom they met in their cross-country walk, all replied in normal tones and in their own tongue. But from looks and gestures Nate assumed that the subject under discussion was someone who looked like Mr. Jackson or was dressed like Mr. Jackson—and where the someone might be found, if at all.

He was not, in fact found at all. But he had left calling cards behind him, as it were.

An air of expectancy hung over all the Land. Far-ven-Sul—the watchers on the cliffs sent back word—it was Far-ven-Sul who had won the right to try to fight the great Red Fish. He, of all the flotilla, Far-ven-Sul! No one could clearly understand how he had come to be with the flotilla at all, for, not only was it not his turn, it was not even his year to try for a turn. It was all most curious, it might even be illegal as well as irregular. Meanwhile, all who could go to watch had gone, and all the rest were waiting—first, for the signal, then for the report, then for the complete description.

The hills were utterly deserted as Nate and Jackson picked their ways through the shale and fallen rocks and timber. Now and then a bird cried out, questioningly, or a tiny creature hopped up upon a boulder or a stump to peer at them briefly before hopping back. And once a grayfowl rocketed up almost from under their feet. Jackson, it seemed plain, was not depending entirely on what he had been able to learn from the locals; was not confined to the limits of this knowledge. He glanced at the lay of the land, examined the rock strata somewhat as though he were a geology student, peered closely at the ground and even audibly sniffed at the air—as though he could hope to see and to smell things which Nate neither smelled nor saw.

Yet, in the end (It was, of course, no end. Mayhap there are no ends at all.) it was Nate who made the discovery.

"Cave," he said, casually, and pointed.

Jackson asked him to stay outside unless or until he was needed and Nate agreed. His clothes were almost dry now and he had some time before replaced his shoes. But both shoes and socks were still a bit damp and so he sat down and removed them once more and spread the socks out on a warm ledge of rock, and devoted a good bit of time to propping up his shoes with twigs and pebbles so as to achieve maximum entrance of sunlight into them. At these harmless tasks he was interrupted by the cries from the cave. The voice sounded like Jackson's, but—perhaps from the amplification and distortion of the cave—it sounded like nothing he had ever heard from Jackson.

No words were intelligible, but the tone and tenor was unmistakable. Alarm. Panic. Fright. Terror.

Nate dropped his shoes and sped into the cave, stooping low. He had almost automatically grabbed up a branch as he ran, and this hit the lintel of the cave, bounding back and then up again before he was able to think about it: then he realized he need no longer stoop. A curious sound or collection of sounds fell upon his ears then—a twittering, chittering, chattering, shrilling sort of thing—perhaps the man, Jackson, had stumbled upon some dangerous creature which lived in the cave, perhaps had been attacked by it. And over this he heard a louder sound, as of gasps of pain.

Cautiously, Nate said, "Jackson . . .? Jackson . . .? You all right?"

His eyes adjusted to the dimmer light and he proceeded down into the cavern. "Jackson?"

"*Jack*-son?"

"*Jackson?*"

He found him at last, leaning against the sloping rock-face and breathing as if each breath hurt him . . . as, indeed, it might: the way he held hands to throat and inclined his head back. He brought his hands *and* his head forward as Nate came up to him and then, with the by-now familiarly odd gesture, he flapped at something on the floor. Something that moved a bit, twitched a bit, moaned a bit.

"You found him, huh. Or . . . I guess . . . he found you, too."

Hoarse and slow and infinitely astonished, Jackson said, "He— He— Tried to take my life."

Nate nodded, not overly surprised, gauged the figure on the floor of the cave to be about Jackson's weight and size. "Well, you seem to have given him a good run for his money."

"You do not under*stand*—" the other's voice rose high, horrified. "He tried to take my *life!* As if I were a different *form* of life!"

"That's an odd way of putting— There's that noise again. What—" Jackson made a late, clumsy move to stop him, but Nate had already glanced in the direction of the sound. A stray, fortuitous beam of sunlight had preceded him, and in its dusty, motey path he saw the sides and top of the rocky chamber covered with, crawling with, alive and pullulating with tiny creatures perhaps an inch long, each. They were six-legged and translucent and wet and shining; skeletal and internal organs showing up, dark, within. And they twittered and they chittered and they chattered.

"See, see what he has also done," Jackson said. He was certainly in a state of shock, and small wonder, Nate thought, feeling his own parts crawl. "He killed the males. He killed the males."

"Sheest, why did he stop there?" Nate said, grimacing. He hefted the branch in his hand. It would do for a club. He raised it and took a step forward. And then Jackson was all over him, grabbing the club, pulling at him, forcing him down, gibbering, hysterical, shrieking. Over and over they rolled, clawing at each other. It was not skill this time, clean or dirty, which enabled Nate to get away, but just sheer luck. Jackson's hold slipped. Nate lunged for the glaring head and thumped it against the rock. The wet gray eyes rolled up. It was with an academic detachment that Nate noted scarcely any lashes on the lids which fluttered, came down.

"Jesus," he said. It was part exclamation, part prayer.

"I'm going to get the hell out of here," he said. Not bothering to do the shoes and stockings bit again, he simply put his head down and charged from the cave.

They were waiting outside for him.

"*There's* the son of a bitch," said the dark young man whom he had left bound up in the Maze on the other side of the City of the Stated Sages; and he fumbled with something Nate recognized as a collapsible carbine.

"Don't do that. *Don't* do that!" ordered the older man who so much resembled him, the man who had said nothing back there at Darkglen, had not even been introduced; who had come in with the laywers Thomas Farrel Smith and John Morton. He had a pistol in his hand, but it was pointing downward. He indicated this with his left hand. "I assume you are armed, Mr. Gordon," he said, crisply. "You disarmed Jack Pace, here—" Jack scowled "—and you would be a fool if you hadn't retained the weapon. I'm sure you are not a fool."

Nate realized, somewhat to his surprise, that he was comparatively glad to see them. In fact, a proverb popped, ready-made into his head. *On Mars, all Earthmen are friends.* And he realized something else, too.

"If I am," he said, "I'm a hungry fool. *I* don't want to fight, at all. It wasn't my idea. You want to talk, I take it. Okay— You got anything to eat? Good! Afterward, I'll tell you what's back in there—" he gestured toward the cave.

"I have some idea. That's why I'm here." He slipped the pistol in a shoulder holster. "My name is Flint. Nicholas. Usually called 'Major.' Break out some rations, Jack. Let's sit down here and keep the mouth of the cave in sight."

Nate watched as Jack sullenly opened a small, square can and smeared its contents on what looked like hardtack. "A new taste sensation," he said, slightly thickly, after a moment, swallowing. "What is it?" he asked.

Major Flint said that it was pemmican. "Dried meat with suet, sugar, and raisin. This other is whole-grain ship's bread or biscuit. Both available, if you know where to look."

'I *thought* it wasn't tuna fish."

Pace flushed and looked daggers at him, but Major Flint was undisturbed. He took out a worn-looking, much mended pipe already stuffed with tobacco, and lit it; then, folding his arms across his chest, he stood where he could keep in sight not only the mouth of the cave but the downward slope of the hill. A look from him, and Pace took his eyes away from Nate and—his weapon still not readied, but in his hands and ready to be readied—set them on the upward slope.

After a short while Nate said, "Okay. Let's talk."

"We engaged those lawyers for you," Major Flint said,

immediately, with a puff of cheap tobacco smoke. "You didn't help matters much by vanishing again like that, but I expect that won't matter. There's a lot more money behind us than that county has ever seen in its entire history. So, forget about that.

"You've caused us a bit of trouble, you know, but I'm prepared to believe it was entirely inadvertent, so we'll forget about that, too. I've been impressed by the fact that you've consistently displayed a quick mind and a quick body. Those are always excellent qualities, no matter what the occasion, but they show up particularly well under circumstances which have been known to set weaker minds and bodies completely off balance. We haven't come looking for you because you represent a menace to us, though. We're here because you represent an asset. A quick-witted young man in first-rate physical and mental shape, one who has had military training and learned discipline, and one who knows something of what this whole wonderful apparatus is all about—just the sort of person we can't have too many of. I know quite a bit about you, Gordon, although you don't as yet know much of anything about me. You want adventure. There's all the adventure anyone could want, waiting for you. You need money. There's already so much of it behind us that I'm a little bit afraid to tell you just how much. And it's hardly possible to conceive how much more is waiting, just to be earned, Gordon. Just to be earned.

"Don't think in terms of common men and common money, Gordon. No. Think in terms of Cortez. Pizzaro. Bonaparte . . . Although he did fail, in the end. We won't. No . . . We won't fail."

Certainly he seemed supremely confident, supremely calm, standing there on the hillside in that alien world. A chill little wind seemed to play up and down Nate's spine as he looked at him and thought of all the implications. *We*, the man had said, and said again, and again. Not just himself and his younger sidesman, obviously.

"We won't, because, for one thing, some of us have been waiting too long to allow ourselves to fail. And because there's too much at stake for all of us for any of us to falter. Great rewards, Gordon, follow great services. *Or ought to*—" Flint's eyes flashed and his right cheek twitched a bit, just a bit, as if he were thinking of great services which had not been rewarded . . . his own, perhaps . . . "I can't think of any greater service, can you?—than saving our country and our race from otherwise certain destruction?"

Nate blinked. He decided not to try to answer what was, obviously, a rhetorical question. He jerked his head back toward the cave.

"What's in there?" he asked.

"*Things*, Gordon. Creatures. Talking dogs. But useful, Gordon. I can tell you that only a fool destroys useful things merely because he doesn't like them."

Somewhere, far down and faraway, a note like that of a great gong sounded and resounded, faint but clear. The three men glanced in its direction, then glanced back. "But . . . what *are* they?"

Jack Pace muttered an obscenity which was probably intended as a definition as well. Nicholas Flint ignored him. "They're called Chulpex. I don't know where the word came from, in its present form; it's been around a long time, though. I think it's an approximation of their name for themselves in their own language. They don't really know how to speak ours, you know—probably you don't know, it's true, though—they just seem to. Somehow. That's one of the things that is going to make them so useful: each one is a ready-made interpreter. And as for their numbers," here the Major chuckled and for the first time he smiled; he fingered his mustache with one finger. "—why, Gordon, the swarming masses of Asia aren't fit to be mentioned in the same breath."

The day had begun to cool, but it still had quite a way to go before being over. Again and again the great and distant gong sounded its deep and melancholy note. It was announcing, though none of the three there up in the hills knew it, the death of Far-ven-Sul in honored combat against the Great Red Fish. No songs would be made about his fight and daring and death, though, unlike any of those which preceded it. He had struck no clever blows, made no clever maneuvers, no brave strokes. He had just died, floundering, bewildered, suddenly at the end screaming in terror. It was scarcely to be understood, another and stupefying, final item in the mystery of how he had come to be the chosen one at all. For he had seemed so confident! True, it was unknown to any of them where he had trained or where he could have trained; it was not his year or turn thereabouts. They had wondered about it, but all took it for granted that he must have trained *somewhere* . . . somewhere unknown to any of them.

No . . . None of them understood. Except, perhaps, the woman Tas-tir-Hella. And she, white-faced and wide-eyed in

her room, would tell no one. Only the reports of his death
and all of that about it, convinced her that all she knew was
neither illusion nor hallucination.

The stranger had promised her the love of Far-ven-Sul if
she would bring him to him. He had promised Far-ven-Sul
the death of the great merfather if Far-ven-Sul would show
him caves which no one else knew of. It did not fit together;
it fit together too well; it had happened; it was not to be
believed. Vaguely, in the agony of grief, Tas-tir-Hella made
up her mind to return at once to her Centrum and ask her
Healer to arrange an amnesia for her.

"Those damn Gooks," Major Flint said, almost benignly
amused, "they think that they are going to outnumber *us*—eh,
Jack?"

Jack tossed his head and snickered.

Nate said, "But . . . won't it be kind of *crowded?*"

A slight trace of annoyance passed over the major's face
like a small cloud swiftly flying over the face of the sun, was
succeeded by the same self-assured expression as before
. . . perhaps even a bit intensified. "Only temporarily. And
not even everywhere," he said.

"There's a bunch of little creeps there in the cave, you
know." Nate Gordon told him. "As for the two big ones
. . . I don't know . . ." He described what had happened.

Pace pursed his lips distastefully. Major Flint gave a little
bit of a shrug. "We'll go in there and see after a while. They
are, after all, so different from us that there's not much we
can do but see. As for the one that Jackson had the argument with, why, as near as I can make out, that one was a
deserter. So it doesn't matter about him. And as for the
Jackson one, hmm, in a way that one was of much more
importance. It was a contact. But contacts should be easy to
make, now that we've got the Darkglen entrance and all its
arms."

He paused. "I can tell you about that. Of course. I must.
For one thing, Gordon, although old Bellamy had considered
making you his heir, that was all that he'd done, you know—
considered it. There was a draft will drawn up. No more.
There's no telling if he would have ever signed it. Anyway,
that wouldn't have been anything you'd have been content to
stick with, I'm sure. The money was all tied up in trusts
intended, I suppose, to last forever. The actual income didn't
amount to a hill of beans, comparatively speaking; just
enough to maintain the house and keep a man alive in it.

Nothing that would appeal to any young and normal man. Do you know, I don't believe he'd even ever had a woman up there!

"But his death was an accident. Too bad, but that's done with.

"A wasted life. An easy, idle, dry, withered-up, withering kind of a life. Imagine someone dedicating himself to sitting on top of a gold mine, never intending to so much as wash a pan of it for color! Well, that was Bellamy."

Nate cleared his throat. "He—uh—he wasn't the only one was he?"

"The only *what?*"

They examined each closely, appraisingly. This time Nate shrugged. "Watcher," he said.

The great gong sounded once more. Its echoes died away into silence. There were no more sounds from it.

"Why . . . No. Of course not."

"But the others are all trying to keep the Chulpex *out.* Your bunch is trying to get them *in.*"

Annoyance, now, did not leave Major Flint's face. "That is what I have been trying to tell you," he said. "The others are fulfilling a role which is purely negative. The human race is stumbling down a steep hill. 'The Bomb!' My God, Gordon! We won't need any *bomb* to polish us off—the way inferior and defective genes are being allowed—'*allowed*'?—encouraged!—to proliferate. Water seeks its own level, doesn't it? Well, it isn't only water. We're interfering with that essential process, Gordon. And unless something is done, *now! Quick!* we are all of us going to perish. Nature meant the human race to be *pure,* Gordon. Strong. Clean. Every man was to be capable of fending for himself and his family. The fit survived. The unfit vanished, taking their damaged and damaging qualities from the bloodstream.

"Nature made this nation, I mean *our* nation, Gordon— meant it to rule, made it to rule. It was heading the right way, expanding on all sides . . . and then . . ." His voice dropped. "Something went wrong. First there was that fool, Banning. Not an American, of course not, though plenty of Americans were fool enough to follow him—Waksman, Salk, I don't count them, they were Jews. Insulin. Wonder drugs. Vaccine. Relief. Welfare. Subsidies. And taxes, taxes, taxes. Communism, socialism, democracy, anarchy—flourishing on all sides. Some little nigger nation like Zamboanga or whatever in the Hell its name is, six miles long and two miles wide, comes into independent existence, and immediately it's

got a *vote,* Gordon! A—damned—*vote!* In that cursed U.N.
It has one vote and the United States of America has one
vote!

"Well . . ." His voice sighed away. "That won't last much
longer. Fortunately, things are going to be changed mighty
soon. We've all of time and space to draw on, you know
that, and we are going to *use* all of time and space to set
things right. And when they are once set to right here, I
don't mean *here*, damn it! in this gum-ball planet of wherever it is—when things are set to rights in our own country,
our own world and time, why, then, Gordon, then . . ."

Pace must have set up his weapon in a flash, for all Nate
saw was the swift movement, then he saw the piece jerk up,
jump back as it fired. Automatically, he dived for the shelter
of the cliff where it overhung the cave. Flint fired twice. And
something came spinning through the air and fell with an
infinitely ugly sound on the loose shale beneath their feet. It
slid down and forward, crackling, dusty, then came to a stop.

Nate heard Pace say, "There's more of them—" Nate
looked at the face staring blindly upward. He did not know
which of them it was, but he knew it was one of Et-dir-Mor's
grandsons.

He dashed out from his shelter. "Cover me, Major—Jack!"
he yelled. "I know the way up behind them!"

He did not look to see if they were doing as he asked, but
the fact of his not getting a bullet in his back seemed to say
that they were. Or maybe he'd just caught them off guard.
He zig-zagged, running low, between rock and tree and rock.
He was out of sight now. He still kept low, but there was no
more shale underfoot to crackle and disclose his progress, so
he curved around and away. And away . . .

Maybe he would be able to find Et-dir-Mor yet. Maybe
not. Or another of his people. Maybe not that, either. At any
rate, he had lied when he said that he knew "the way up
behind them." He didn't know it at all, didn't even know if
there was such a way at all.

He had, after all, never been there. But he had kept his
eyes open, wide open, well open, and he was pretty confident
that he knew the way to where he had been. He headed
there.

Once, twice, three times, after a while, he looked back.
Once, and twice, he saw nothing, saw no one. The third time
he saw three figures. The two ahead and together would be
Flint and Pace. The third, by the odd gait of it, would be the
thing which was masquerading as a man named Jackson.

He, Nate, still had a fine, good lead on them. With any kind of luck, he should reach the waterfall well before they did.

Darius Chauncey sounded off with a long string of prime, choice Union Army oaths, gliding off at the end into Minoan, Mycenaean, Philistine and Phoenician. "Hell Fire!" he said at last, comparatively tamely—and glared at Nate with a measure of resentment. "I knowed there'd be trouble if I let you in here, into my nice, peaceful pretty-place."

Nice, peaceful, pretty, it certainly was there; the courtyard divided between sunlight and shade, a huge old fig tree in the center of it, vines like pythons crawling up around the sides of the great pillars. The woman who had spread the table with bread and fish and honey and oil and olives and fresh-roasted meat and fruits had seated herself on a stone bench and played softly on a three-stringed instrument. A naked child leaned against her and listened. It occurred to the guest that Darius Chauncey, instead of being the large-scale, free-style lecher he had given himself out to be, might instead have become quite domesticated. He thought he'd work on those lines to start.

"Well, for one thing . . . *cum-raid* . . . *I* didn't make the trouble. You take my word for the rest of it, take my word for that. And for another thing . . . *cum-raid* . . . how much longer do you think it's going to go right on being a 'nice, peaceful pretty-place,' if those lunatics get away with what they're after? The fact that they intend to take over my world in a way which would make Vicksburg seem like a temperance picnic, this may not be any hair off *your* balls: granted. It wouldn't even affect—maybe—your own old world if you ever decided to go back to it.

"But, oh, Brother Chauncey, use your head! It isn't true that access to any gate in the Maze means access to the whole Maze, no. Because some of the ways are blocked up one way or another. But can't you just imagine what would happen if the Chulpex succeed in bypassing the way they've got to go until now? If they get access to an arm of the Maze which has no Watchers? It would be like a game of checkers, and who'd make the moves and jump the men and sweep the board clean? Right! I don't have to tell you about them, that they are not human in anything but intelligence, that there are more of them than we could count if we spent our lives at it, that— You *know* this! Isn't that why you're a

Watcher? Let them get enough of their numbers through, anywhere, and then they can spread out in all directions.

"And eventually, Cum-raid Chauncey, they would come *here*."

His host shifted uneasily on his bench, muttered, glanced around him quickly. His eyes rested for a moment on woman and child. She seemed to sense this, looked up and smiled, then went on with her playing. The music was quite strange to Nate Gordon, but after a while it began to catch his ear and take hold of him and linger.

"Shucks," Chauncey said, in a lower tone; "if they'd ever come into Crete we'd of read about it in the books—wouldn't we?"

Nate shook his head, violently. "Don't cling to that hope," he said, insistently. "That's a straw. Ordinary common-sense applications of the laws of time and space don't apply to the Maze. Maybe this Crete isn't the Crete of our own history at all. No, no—

"Furthermore, it's not the Chulpex alone. There's this fanatic who calls himself Major Flint, him and his band of brothers, whoever they may be. They think they're going to use the Chulpex to do most of their dirty work; then—they think—they'll, somehow, get rid of them. And of course the Chulpex have got exactly the same notion, only in reverse. Suppose that Flint and his men *do* win? He made it; I can tell you, clear enough to me that once they'd conquered the old home world in my time-period and his, that then they'd turn their attention to the rest of time and space."

Chauncey said, "Son of a *bitch*." He got up and stamped the stones of the courtyard, whirled around to face Nate. "Now what in the name of God can I *do?*" he demanded. "I've got this de-vice, you've seen it, long-long thing with a short crosspiece, I don't know exactly how it works—fact is, I don't know how it works at all—but it sure scares the piss out of them Chulpex and sends them packin', fast. Want I should stand there, like Horatius at the Bridge, standin' off the Chulpex Grand Army? I can try. Might work, might not. But you say, suppose they git them some ways out of their own world, they bypass all the watched ways—what do I do then? Come out after 'em, wherever they be, all 'levendy-six skillion of 'm, wavin' my magic sword? You think it'd do a precious lot of good?

"I git along well enough here and now. I come here with a good trick or two up my sleeve, never mind what; and I made me enough to buy some land and a boat. I ain't

disliked much. But even was I to mobilize this whole blessed
island, why, what good would *that* do? These people kin kill
a bird on the wing with a slingshot at a hunderd steps, I seen
'em do it. Think that'd help ag'inst your schools and schools
of Chulpex? How much good would swords or bows and
arrows do in the face of whatever big guns they got in your
day? Why, brave though these people be, brave enough, a
hunderd Minie-balls 'd scatter 'm. You ought to know that
much."

After a moment he said, "I got to think about this."

He walked off, walked up and down, hand on chin. Nate
got up and stretched. He had some thinking to do, himself.
So far, coming here had accomplished nothing, but he had
not known where else to go. Evidently Flint's men had hold
now of the Darkglen entrance, and even if they hadn't and
despite his glib assurances to Nate, Nate felt no certainty of
not being picked up on a murder charge. If indeed a tentative
will in his own favor had been drawn up by old Mr. Bellamy, its existence might well serve only to accuse him of
having had a motive for killing the old man. "You might
have thought it had been signed," they could say.

He was by no means sure of finding the way to Et-dir-Mor
via the Maze, and by no means sure of not finding Flint's
men in possession at that old man's place, either. He thought
he could reach Chauncey, though—as he had done—and they
two at least shared a common language and, up to a point, a
common history and pattern of thought.

Nate stretched again, and yawned. He had expended
enough energy, Lord knew, to justify fatigue; and, too, this
last meal had helped make him drowsy. A hand touched his
arm. It was the woman, Chauncey's wife or whatever she
was. Strange, strange, she was no longer playing her kithara
or whatever it was, because the tune was still going through
his head. She smiled, imitated his yawn, gestured toward the
room off the courtyard, bent over and patted an invisible
bed.

"Might's well catch forty winks if you can and want to,"
Chauncey said, stopping in his perplexed walk back and
forth. "I'll wake you if I think of anything. *Thun*deration."

The bed was made with straw and sheepskins with the
fleeces still on them. Nate dropped off his shoes and his
heavy, heavy coat, and crawled in with a groan. Straw and
skins alike smelled vividly and he was commiserating with
himself for not being able to fall asleep when, with a start of

surprise too strong not to waken him, he fleetingly realized that he already had.

It was dark when he awoke, a darkness relieved by a huge fire and a multitude of twinkling little oil lamps. Darius Chauncey loomed against the firelight. He rose when he saw Nate, picked up two of the tiny earthen vessels with their burning, smoldering wicks. "Help yourself to a couple," he said, "and come along . . .

"They ain't a Hell of a much good," he conceded. "From time to time I have thought of trying my hand at producing some summer-strained whale oil, glass chimbleys, a good woven and adjustable broad wick: modern, up-to-date inventions, as it were. But it's for one thing ag'inst the unwritten rules, and then, too, I says to myself, 'D'ri—just don't you rock the boat.' So I haven't. Not so much as a tallow candle. Them few tricks I had up my sleeve, never mind what, they don't count.

"Step down here. Step down . . ."

He set his lamps on a table in a chamber walled all in stone, and put the two that Nate carried on the other side, one in each corner. He pointed to something in the center, something like a small and truncated pyramid of translucent stone. "Know what that is?" he asked, gesturing. The lines of light, finer than spiderwebs, gleamed and did their strange gleaming things in the dim lamplight.

Nate nodded. "It's a ward or a ward-stone. Et-dir-Mor told me a bit about it. He had one, too, of course. And—oh-oh!—now that I come to think of it . . . so do I . . . in . . . my . . . pocket . . ."

He stared at Chauncey, who stared back. Just as Nate's voice had, word by word, fallen lower, so now the other's grew word by word louder as he repeated, "You've got one—in . . . your . . . *pocket?* How—"

Nate told him how he had found it under Joseph Bellamy's body, how he had taken it with him when first he ventured into the strange world-between-worlds which was the Maze. "Eventually, I suppose, I just stuck it into my pocket and forgot about it."

"Just . . . forgot about it. Well, if that don't beat the Dutch. Never mind," he said, abruptly. "Pay attention now to what I'm about to show you, and try to learn awful damn quickly. Pick it up. Hold it so. No—*so*. Like that. There, now, you let it drop a trifle. Up . . . over . . . See how the lines swell when you do it thataway? *All* right. Now—"

Nate said, "What's this for, that you're trying to teach me?"

Chauncey sighed and sighed. "You maybe won't thank me, and I may be doing wrong. But I'm going to show you how to reach the Center. And when you git there, well, you just tell the Masters all that you've been telling me. Maybe they'll help you. I know they *kin*. What I don't know, I don't know if they *will*."

His speech, in voice and accents, had sounded old-fashioned and comforting. It was like hearing, somehow, the archetypal American Old Man, somehow grown young. But when his voice stopped and Nate looked at him, bare-waisted and bronzed and kilted in the light of the flickering tiny lamps, he saw nothing but what belonged, seemingly, to the strange and alien world of Minoan Crete. And as for what he had been saying—

" 'Center?' 'Masters?' The Center and the Masters of *what*?" he asked, bewildered. Again the strange tune of the strange stringed instrument ran through his mind, but it brought him no comfort.

"Why," said Darius Chauncey, slowly, "of the Maze, of course . . . of the whole, entire, wonderful, damnable Maze . . ."

CHAPTER NINE

The Quechuas had trotted past him in a steady stream and at a steady pace. Some carried baskets or boxes by themselves, or were two-men teams carrying bales upon poles. Three men went by, one after the other, bent at increasing angles beneath the weight of elaborately engraved sun-disks of increasing size. Once a file of six men loped by, holding up the links of an enormous and glittering chain. Now and then one of the Quechuas, no more, would turn his eyes to look at him from the corners—a quick, quick, fearful glance— then they were gone. And once a noble in gorgeous regalia had gone by, swiftly, in a palanquin, face composed and

frozen in almost unbelief, his eyes glassy with the shock of a
man whose god is captive.

"Don't bother, do not bother, hide your treasures and flee
to the cloud-covered cliffs or the clamorous jungles," Nate
had wanted to tell them. "It will do no good; those you think
to placate worship a god who was killed and in whose name
they will, nevertheless, kill your god."

But he had not said it. They could not have understood
him, they would not have believed him. With deliberate
speed, bowed down with grief and gold, they hastened to fill
the insatiable chamber which held the Inca Atahualpa.

Fortunately no Spaniards passed his way. He followed the
arrow-straight, stone-paved road which went up and went up;
then he turned aside along a winding and probably pre-Incan
trail which vanished into mists so cold he was glad of still
having his overcoat. He had at one point grown hungry, but
this was no problem: he stopped at the first roadside meal he
saw in progress, and pointed. Bowing low, the men handed
him the grilled ribs and baked potatoes; he walked on as he
ate; behind him they murmured, "*Viracocha . . . Viracocha . . .*"

He walked slowly, slowly up the outer steps of the vast
and crumbling and deserted temple he found at last, and
down and down, down, down the inner steps. It grew gradually so dark that it was not until he chanced to blink and
the skin of his face flashed into paroptic sight that he realized he had re-entered the Maze. He closed his eyes and
walked straight across and through the dancing minotaurs
and opened his eyes and came to an outside again where it
was dark but not perfectly dark. Dimly, he saw that he was
in a narrow place confined on either side by walls. It stank
terribly of stale urine and there was the ugly noise of many,
many angry or frightened people some distance away. He
paused to consult his ward.

Far off on one of the edges was a thin line of light which
was nonetheless thicker than the other lines. He had come
far, and come far in a way and manner not susceptible to
any means of measurement he knew of; he was terribly tired,
he was frightened and oppressed; but now at last the Center
was beginning to come into sight, and he could not stop.

He went on.

The great open place he next came to was paved with slabs
of stone both slippery and uneven. There was not a soul in
sight. He looked up and was just able to make out a great,
pagodalike tower when the night exploded at his left into

light and sound. A torrent swept across the square, guided by torch-flare, a torrent of shouting men whose dark faces gleaming with sweat and angry ecstasy were framed in long black hair barely confined by red headbands. Nate Gordon did not know the name of the city, nor the date within a decade; but in that glimpse he knew that the Taipings had entered the city; that was enough. He ran, he fled.

And the adherents of the Great Peace ran after him, shouting their joy and fervor and holy zeal and hatred, desirous only of taking his head and laying it at the feet of the Heavenly Wang, the potent Younger Brother of Jesus the Son of God.

Nate ran, flying and moaning, across the square and then down past the first, second, and the third hutungs; but then he had to go slow and to grope. He was gone by the time the torches reached there, but it made no difference: One may begin at any point in taking the measure of a circle, and the city was justifiably doomed in any event. Such of the women who were young and not ugly and had not perfidiously hanged themselves with their sashes, the victors saved, however, that the Heavenly Wang might take his choice of them and grace them by ascension to his terrestrial couch.

The mead was all a-flower with golden asphodel as Nate plodded across it with head hanging and feet dragging, barely noticing the perfume of them.

"Yonder comes Nathaniel," said the first fair woman. "It is in vain that you pursue the horizon, Nathaniel. If you concern yourself with violence, you will become violent. There is no way through the mire which will not cause you to become miry. All is illusion, is it not, sisters?—all except my house, my palace, the name of which is Wisdom. There are seven times seven gates, and I will lead you through all of them in the proper order, and thus you will in time grow wise and know the proper course of things, not wasting time and substance in vain pursuit— Is it not so, sisters?"

He lifted the small, truncated pyramid of the dawn-colored ward-stone and peered at the mesh of luminous golden lines, but his eyes blurred and the lines blurred with them. He blinked and squinted, but it did no good.

"It is *not* so," the second fair woman said, her voice ringing like a quickened bronze. "You will teach him to be at peace; he has no right to be at peace while any are at war. Go back, Nathaniel! Go back! Darius has only placed his burden upon you and sent you off with it into the wilderness;

it is nothing to him if the weight of it causes you to be dashed in pieces. Do not continue this retreat, do not engage in speculation equally vain, return and fight, Nathaniel! Return and fight! Return—and I will go with you and fight by your side— Shall I not, sisters?"

The little wind danced across the field, and all the golden flowers briefly bowed their heads. Nate tried to speak, but his lips were dry and his throat was raw.

"No, you shall not," the third fair woman said. "You would not remain, you never remain. Besides, he shall not go with you. Nathaniel. Nathaniel. There is always a menace. There is always a war. It is futile to become engaged, as futile as to try the impossible escape of introspection. Leave them and come with me, Nathaniel, for I can take you to a point beyond the circle, to a time before time, a place only to be reached through me. We will be pre-Adam and pre-Eve, Nathaniel; god and goddess, Nathaniel; Shelomo and Shulamith, Solomon and Sulamite. On me, Nathaniel, you will beget a new race which need never fall into the errors of any of the old ones . . .

"Come *with* me, Nathaniel—"

"Come with *me*—"

"*Come with me*—"

"Come . . ."

He sat down on the fragrant ground and let the little wind ruffle his hair. When he looked up again, they were gone. He arose and trudged on and by and by he sighted the Lion Gate and he passed beneath its carven, stony lintel.

The next place was all black and white and something sniffed and snuffled and scuffled up ahead and made a noise of dragging fur and of scrabbling claws. Something very big. Something shadowy.

Nate turned around and softly went past and beyond and behind the way he had come in; then he went around. He did not look back.

Now the arms of the Maze shuttled back and forth and in and out, like great flashings. He paused and listened intently, holding his breath. Everything stopped. He did not move. Six paces ahead of him, where he would have been had he moved, two surfaces came together in an annihilating crash. *Then* he moved. And passed through safely. Behind him, the wrack continued. Ahead all was serene.

The man in the ragged turban addressed him in a French so odd and warbling that no Frenchman could have understood it. "Turn back," he urged. "Turn back, O Ferenghi. For all that you must have embraced *Al-Islam*, or you would not dare to venture here, what will that avail you? There is cholera the length and breadth of the road to Mecca, *hadji* and *ulema* alike crawl upon their bellies like dogs in hopes of dying in the Sacred City. Turn back, O Ferenghi. There will be time enough for you to try the *haj* again. Has not the sultan's *capidan*-pasha defeated the *giaours* at Lepanto? Turn back! Turn back!"

The frightful sun beat down upon them. Nate shook his head, and staggered on. His overcoat upon his arm sank down as though filled with stones.

The man in the ragged turban tottered on beside him. "Let not it be said that your death was on my head," he pleaded. "Return at least to Jiddah, where there are other foreigners, and lodge there until the plague be stayed."

Nate said, "No . . ."

"The brigand tribes are harrying the pilgrims like wolves. Those in the caravans are not safe; how then shall a single man on foot hope to escape?"

Nate said nothing. He put his hand to his forehead. He went on.

"*Wellah!*" cried the man. "There is water, the last for leagues and leagues. Will you not at least pause and drink and gain strength?"

"No," said Nate.

The would-be guide threw up his hands. "This is caution thrice compounded," he moaned. "Do you fear that the cholera has got into that little spring? It may be so. Stop—Stop for just a moment." He fumbled in his robe, took out a leather bottle. "Here is water as pure as water ever was. I filled it at the Holy Well of Zam-Zam near the Kaaba, before leaving Mecca. The plague had not reached there. For the sake of the merit, I will share it with you. Drink, my brother. Drink, or you must die."

Nate shook his head. The man in the tattered turban grasped hold of him and thrust the wet, cool mouth of the water bottle to Nate's parched and foul-tasting mouth. Nate shouldered him aside, the man stumbled, the bottle fell with gentle slowness so that at any moment he could have reached out and seized it, righted it. He went on. The bottle hit the sand with a thud. Water splashed, gurgled, was gone. By his side the man looked with sickened incredulity. The skin of his face stretched over an empty skull in which burned the two *ghul*-bright eyes of Shaitan the Accursed. And then he was gone, and the desert sands blew through his robe and rags.

In the middle distance the sun of fire blazed up from the walls of long-hidden Iram, the City of Brass. That way Nate followed on his burning feet.

He passed on, from outside to outside, down endless corridors echoing with the witless whistlings of the mindless minotaurs, through gate after gate. He ceased to see places. He experienced conditions and states. Nausea that racked him without ceasing. Hunger which bit him in every sense and cell. Vertigo, making mockery of such illusions as *up* and *down*. Cold such as had never numbed man before, surely, without having killed him. He could barely hold the wardstone, scarcely see through frozen eyes. But up from the meshy weave of pulsing lines shone the tiny not-yet disk of the Center. He was not really near it. But he was perceptibly less far away.

The ward looked quite good on his table. The room was warm. He had dined well, there was a drink within reach, the manuscript in the typewriter was coming along just fine. He might have to tone it down a bit, but in general his description of the hashish-dream was calculated to convince any editor or reader who had never smoked or eaten hashish. It was, in fact, so vivid, that it almost for a moment had convinced Nate. Vast areas of it, blossoming like an evil flower, in the mind of his imagination, had not even reached the paper yet. Probably never would. There wasn't room.

He paused in his attack on the keyboard, stretched pleasurably. If some of the details escaped while he was doing so, never mind. He had plenty. There were just a few more pages. In fact, there were only a few more fictional-factual articles to go. And then, with his $4,000 in bank drafts, travelers checks, and plain old dirty cash money, he could kiss the local scene good-bye and take off for Coimbra, Calabria, Carpathia, Carniola, and all the rest of it, pausing a bit to kick a fallen leaf in Vallimbrosa. Some particular detail—as was so often the case—nagged and tugged against being forgotten. Piss on it. A writer had to be firm, when the spirit was upon him like this, not to stop and allow this to happen, or else he would be overwhelmed. Still, it could be annoying. He must be firm.

Being firm, he got up to go to the bathroom. In the past he had found this often to be more helpful in forgetting than he could wish. Being firm, he knew that if he looked out the window he would forget important threads of his narrative.

So he looked out the window and, by an immense effort of concentration, he recognized the two men casually coming up the street.

Jack Pace and Major Flint.

The apartment and street ceased to be. He was, like one of his own characters, on the face of a cliff. He turned and began to clamber up the rocky wall. The *ping* of a bullet sounded. Powdered rock spurted into his face. He shouldered his way into a cleft in the rocks. Outside, something swooped on leathery wings and breathed its rage at him out of a huge triangle of teethy, stinking mouth. He put his back to the rock behind him, pushed, inched up. And up. And up. Soon there was nothing behind to press and lever against. He had to grope and climb. A looming shadow warned him in time enough to squirm around and kick out. The claws at the wing tip ripped at him. The creature fell away below, eddied there a moment, flapped away. He had no doubt it would be back. *Sping—ping!*

He turned his defenseless back and climbed with bleeding, splintered fingernails. The tiny pterodactyls bit and gibbered at him in their noisome nest. He kicked them aside and burrowed through the filthy, foul, unbelievably foul mass of clotted dung and bones and dirt. One hand reached free, reached through. Able to close his eyes, trying to breath through his mouth, he heard the parent-thing land on the ledge. He gave a great, desperate lunge. Behind him, the tunnel in the guano collapsed with a dusty thud. The pterodactyl clucked its disconsolate confusion.

Nate looked at his guide. The rosy tint was fainter, the violet one deeper. He had never seen the disk of the Center fullface, of course, or even anything near it. But he had seen it grow from a line to a thin spindle. And now, now as he looked, there could be no doubt. The spindle had grown thinner.

He had somewhere taken a wrong turning. He was heading away from, not toward, the Center.

He turned in his tracks. He stopped. If he turned his clothes inside out, or even if he didn't, the stench didn't matter—they'd serve as a pillow. He could rest a little. A little would suffice. It made no sense to think of "losing time."

There could be no question of that, not when *time* meant no more than *space*. There were no such constants. The only constants were the needs of his own body. It required food, it required rest. If he went on, he could not go on. This was the simplest equation.

But he had to go on!

He picked up his feet, took another reading, and started to start off again. Then he stopped. Ahead, far, far ahead, crossing his corridor at right angles, in steady single file, was a line of the tiny creatures he had seen in the cave in Red Fish Land. That is . . . no, of course: it was only the distance which made them appear tiny. If they were that tiny he would not be able to see them at all. Therefore, it followed that they must be full size.

Chulpex.

Part of an old proverb came into his mind. *If you can't go across, you must go around* . . .

Wearily, wearily, he turned and walked away again, in the wrong direction which was now and for the moment of the foreseeable present-future the right direction.

All the costumes were strange to his smarting eyes, but it was apparent that there was a wide variety of types, both of costumes and of people. Some glanced at him, but no one seemed more than mildly interested. Among those who were engaged to that degree at least, was a woman of white hair and erect carriage. She gave him a quizzical glance.

" 'How dear to my heart are the scenes of my childhood,' " she said; adding, "Not really, though . . . Still, if I may be of help? I come from your future, if you want to put it that way. You do stink," she said, not offensively.

The pathway of the Maze seemed to shine faintly underneath the great stone slabs. Warm sun, blue sky.

"Match you, quote for quote," he offered, wearily. " 'And I have promises to keep . . .' Also, not that it matters, 'Where am I?' "

Nodding, she gathered up the rich folds of her robe. "You're in one of the several cities called Tarshish. Atlantis sank not very long ago. Almost everyone got away, though. Proto-Basques, for the greater part. That's how I happened to come here. Linguist, you know. Glotto-chronology, to be precise. My paper would create the proverbial furor in academic circles, only of course I shan't ever go back to write it. I don't intend to keep up with you," she said, slowing her steps. "Your promises are not mine. But if you ever return,

young man, and want to see me, ask for the House of the
Golden Bull. It's the biggest whorehouse on the coast, and I
run it. A gift for languages and a firm grasp of double-entry
bookkeeping are the secrets of my success. Bye-bye . . ."

The golden-glowing lines of the Mazeway led him straight
into a grass-grown heap of slab near some old tin smelteries.
He went on through and it was on an island in an oily sea,
whose air reeked of iodine and sulphur and whose sky was
smeared with the tail of a tremendous comet, that someone
rose to bar his way.
    Curiously, he felt much less tired now.
    "Bigot," said the other. "Chauvinist."
    "How so?" Nate asked.
    "You come from a world racked with national and racial
and religious and class hatreds. You cannot think these are
good things."
    "I don't," said Nate. "So why do you call me those
names?"
    "You have condemned with almost no personal knowledge
or experience a form of life different from your own, and on
no better grounds than that it is a form of life different from
your own. Therefore: bigot. Therefore: chauvinist."
    The rufous sky burned and smouldered. Something lay,
half-in, half-out the oily sea, and beat its lacey pseudopods
upon the argent gravel of the beach. The other who con-
fronted and addressed him was in appearance and even
sound infinitely less humanoid than the Chulpex were—squat
and lowly and coarsely cellular, with external pouchings like
honeycomb tripes—gruff and smacking in its tone—but he
stopped and considered what the other said. "This isn't quite
true, you know," said Nate. "I . . . 'condemn' . . . them
just as I condemn their allies of my own species."
    The figure smacked its contempt for this defense. "It is
quite true that you condemn on the evidence of members,
no: one single member of your own species: the one called
Flint: whom you also condemn. Is this logic? Is this rational
thought?"
    "You've got somewhat of a point there," Nate admitted.
"But don't forget that there's also the evidence of Et-dir-Mor
and his family—"
    "That will not do!" Wetly, gruffly, the other brushed this
defense aside. "Has Et-dir-Mor and his family met the entire
race? Have they met most of that race? Could they, in the
nature of things, have met more than a fraction of any entire

race? They could not and you must know that they could
not! Yet you condemn all. May it not be that they have met
only those of that race who, for reasons of their own, have
chosen to lie? It may be so, and, indeed, in the absence of
any evidence to the contrary, you ought to assume it is
so."

Nate considered this a while. Then, nodding, he said,
"Very well. I will assume that it is so. I could say, then, I
condemn only those whose actions appear at only one remove to be worthy of condemnation. And if condemnation
ought not—and I am now ready to concede it ought not—
ever to be done at even one remove, then I will say that I do
not condemn any. I renounce any distaste which I have felt
which may have been based either on physical dissimilarity
or on ways and practices possibly based on things unknown
to me, and which I ought not without much greater study to
denounce."

The other said, "This is well, the man. Then you will give
over your project of enmity and return to your own time and
place, ready to give fair consideration to any of another
species who may appear among you."

Nate said, "No."

He said, "My project can no longer be said to be one of
enmity. It is now one of inquiry, only. You may be right in
all that you imply, as well as all that you say. On the plane
of abstract logic, that is, you may be right. But life-forms do
not and cannot exist for more than a moment on that plane;
they must exist in and on the plane of life, and life and logic
are not one. If you are indeed right, then I ought to go on in
order to be convinced that you are right by those who are
my superiors in knowledge and in wisdom. If you are wrong
. . . then they, I hope, will tell me what is right."

The other growled and gurgled its disapprobation. "You
'hope!' Suppose yours is a vain hope? Suppose you are deceived? Has any ever made this same journey and returned
in peace to tell of it? May not this whole Maze be no more,
indeed, than the web of some megamorphous spider, as it
were?"

Nate sighed, looked at the great and burning comet spread-
ing its tail like some celestial peacock all across the alien sky,
amid which meteors like burning embers melted down from
the alien heavens. "I do not know," he said. "I am beset by
uncertainties. There are no certainties at all which any longer
seem of any use to me. But to turn in my tracks after a jour-

ney of such length and such dangers seems to me to be less sensible than to continue. And I bid you now farewell."

And the disk blazed by now three-quarters full.

The living crystals of the Moons of Lor called out and sang to him in wonder. Great, striped marsupial dogs of a nameless, manless world howled and bayed as they tracked him down a narrow, golden gorge. He rose, slowly, wreathed in bubbles, through the warm, fresh waters of an inland, island-studded sea. Trilobites crawled about and nuzzled his tracks. The painted men of Morner hissed and nudged each other as he passed their way, and sent their armed and armored panderers padding after him, down the perfumed streets. But even these cried out in horror as he, following the ever-brighter golden tracks which glowed beneath his feet for him alone, escaped them by vaulting the bridge across the victim-pits and darting into the shallow dens where the paragryphons lounged and preened. The men in armor winced, fearing almost as much as they feared their masters, the screams and flurries which—to their bemusement forever after—never came.

He came out upon a vast plain of wider horizons than he had ever seen, its turf plucked smooth as velvet by great grazing flocks of squat and scarlet birds tended by dwarfs with staves. These clucked and muttered their amusement to see him suddenly stop and glance behind them; then they whistled shrilly and rounded up their flocks and fled with them to safety in the great rounded pens of silent stone dotting the plain. Behind him and to the right and to the left of him, in a vast and terrifying crescent, came the Chulpex in their hundreds of thousands, their clamor as they sighted him rising high and shrill. The crescent swept forward, closed in, swept closer. The massed, rank, raw stink of them struck him in the face. He choked, stumbled, crawled for a space upon his hands and knees. But when they had formed a circle and began to move in from the circumference, he was not to be found.

But, given a specific and limited area, and a large—a very, very large—number of intelligent beings under a discipline both instinctive and trained, a point within that area will sooner or later be found.

So, sooner or later, they found it.

But by then Nate was back in Red Fish Land.

He was, of course, in a way, happy to see Et-dir-Mor

again. The High Physicist looked a decade older, and his surviving twin grandson had aged as well. But—

"I can't be back here again!" Nate cried. "Am I out of my mind? I can't have been going in the wrong direction all this time again. I left this place behind me—"

He stopped, for a moment trembling on the verge of hysteria. And then, in a single second, it left him. Understanding took its place. He smiled. "Evidently," he said, "paradox is a fundamental principle of the Maze." He looked at Et-dir-Mor's ward-stone. The Center was nowhere to be seen. He looked at his own ward-stone. The blazing circle of its sun was almost full. "Paradox," he repeated. "A fundamental principle of the Maze . . ."

Et-dir-Mor nodded. In a low voice he said, "It may even be that the Et-dir-Mor and the Red Fish Land you see now are not the same as those you saw before. I said once to Nathaniel Gordon . . . perhaps, indeed, to you; perhaps to one who is now only at the start of his quest—I do not know—that the Maze crosses dimensions, times, sections, sectors, parallels and places, and things for which we have neither name nor conception nor capacity."

"It crosses paradoxes, too."

Someone struck with a staff the pillar of sounding wood at the outer gate, and was on his way in before the resonant echo of it had gone away. "I must be on my way, in any case," Nate said, getting to his feet.

"Not so fast, young man," said the newcomer.

Et-dir-Mor's lined face brightened. "Am-bir-Ros!"

"Let a fellow countryman take a gander at you before you take off again," the newly arrived old man said, smoothing his white mustachios. "Yes . . . You're one of that ugly race of homo saps, all right. I can hardly stand looking at you; too much sugar for a penny. Ugh. Brr." He shook his head like a dog. "Ambrose Bierce, late of the United States Army, the fourth estate, the State of California, and all the rest of that nasty nonsense. Tell me," he haid, abruptly; "do you still have God back there?"

"Yes . . . I guess we do."

Bierce made a noise in his throat. "The Old Testament one?"

"Some say so."

"The great, mighty, and terrible God who made Heaven and earth? The God of wrath, the God of vengeance, the jealous God, 'the Lord is a man of war, the Lord is His name?' *That* God?"

"Some say so," said Nate.

"Only God that makes any sense," Bierce said, reflectively, suddenly calm. "That's where Mrs. Eddy's soothing science made its first big mistake. She kept confusing Him with Lydia Pinkham . . . Good-bye, young fellow. Good luck. I'd ask you if there's still a G.A.R. in your America, but I'm afraid of what the answer would be."

The corridor sloped so steeply that he had to lean backward. It was so hot that he had discarded the last of his clothing. True, for all he knew, he might next find himself in the roaring middle of a Fimbul-blizzard. But . . . somehow . . . he did not think so. Nor was he altogether surprised when he came to the place whence issued the clanging and banging which had been growing stronger and louder. The ground leveled out, and he saw the giants ahead of him. Twenty feet tall and more, they towered, made of jointed iron in which their molded muscles stood out, and sweat like oil streamed down their faces, flanks, and limbs. Faces contorted with their effort, each in his turn raised far over iron head an iron flail . . . poised it there a moment . . . brought it down upon the ground. He was in the courtyard of the Castle of Vergil the Nigromancer.

They did not beat the floor in unison, though, or anything like it. Nate stood stock-still, admiring the spectacle, but all the while his brain was storing up information. He did not, as on an earlier and somewhat similar occasion, dash across. He walked. Flails crashed behind and before him, shaking the ground, shaking the air. He walked, now slowly, now swiftly, he never stopped, and presently the noise died away behind him. Vergil sat at his desk in wide-eyed sleep, leaning upon his book, and his visitor did not disturb him. Only the hound at the sorcerer's feet twitched and growled a bit without awakening.

The great glowing sun filled almost all the ward-stone, with only a few lines left, like an aureole, around it.

It had been so long since he had heard any noise except the small sound of his feet, that his mind did not at first clearly register or clearly report what—suddenly, retroactively—he became aware of having been subliminally aware of for . . . how long? . . . he did not know. Nor did he know what it was. Only that there seemed to be and to have been a whispering. Looking around, looking back, he saw nothing. A sound increasing to the sound of a wind, perhaps, strong enough to rustle the leaves of a tree. But he felt no wind. There was no tree.

The noises multiplied, increased, became nasty little noises, became frightful, frightening little noises. The things which made them scuttled and lurched across the very periphery of his vision, and the scant, abrupt glimpses he could catch of them before they vanished made him shudder. They stank, these things, these abominable things making the abominable sounds, not in any familiarly noisome fashion, but in a way which simultaneously wrenched his stomach and buffeted his mind. His mouth gagged, his tongue fell in revulsion away from the palate. Parts of his body began to crawl and twitch, inside and out; pain assaulted him, and sickness, in muscles and organs of whose existence he had never been before reminded by so much as slight discomfort. His skin prickled, his face fell into a frozen grimace, and the drums of his ears trembled and shuddered in fear.

The things were getting inside of him even more, they had gotten inside his body, now they were getting inside his mind. He could see them and smell them and taste them in his skull now, their gromly noises were both muffled and heard more acutely, as they flopped and hunched and squirmed their way along the convolutions of cerebrum and cerebellum. No sensation of feeling had ever been anything like this. Pain? It transcended pain, it was the sickness unto death, and in a short time he was surely going to die—die from the sheer shock of this horror. His heart lurched in the grip of the titan fist which squeezed it, his breast was pierced with arrows.

There was only one escape. If he could cut off the communication of his senses, he could rest and gather strength. If he could, for just the shortest time, cease to relate, to be aware, find refuge in himself alone . . .

If he could go mad . . .

This, of course, was what was wanted. But it was not he who wanted it: it was *they!*

Nate opened his eyes and the blaze of glory which was the Maze in that moment fell into blackness, and in that blackness he neither saw nor heard nor smelled nor tasted. For a moment he still continued to feel. But for a moment, only. Then his body was merely weak and trembling, and he felt only the things which it was fit to feel. He walked along like a blind man without a staff, his hands touching one wall. And when, after one hundred thousand years, he felt it yield, he turned and went on through.

He lurched against the dirty gilt decorated side of a sedan chair, he went down and it went over. The yellow-faced, mustached woman inside of it tore at the masses of rusty black lace which slipped over her eyes and began to scream a long long scream, with lots of palatal sounds and glottal stops. But Nate had not fallen nor had the sedan chair gone over because he had lurched against it. Everything was falling, all was going down: the towering slums running up the hills like scabby serpents, the masked mansions of the Hidalgos and the coats of arms hanging over them, the ornate baroque gingerbread churches, the foreign consulates, wine warehouses, the Palace of the Inquisition . . .

Some ran through the buckling streets crying out that it was the end of the world, others knelt upon the heaving earth to pray their sorrow and contrition for their sins; others yet, maddened for the moment into forgetfulness of the Inquisition, seemed to have thought and word only to take the advice of Job's wife: *Curse God and die* . . . And there were those who seemed not to think of themselves but only of tearing with their fingers at the rubble beneath which protruding and broken, bleeding limbs yet twitched and jerked. The lead chairman was one of these, and so, perhaps surprisingly, was the sallow widow he and his flight fellow a moment ago were bearing through the streets of Lisbon; together they toiled and pried and pulled, she never for a moment leaving off screaming.

But most of the people paused neither to pray nor curse nor aid others: they streamed toward the great, broad quay in the harbor. No buildings were there to topple over and crush them; here, on the contrary, were ships to carry them to safety. Thither, then, unto the port they fled, in their hundreds and their thousands and, at last, their many scores of thousands. There, too, must Nate have gone, because it was there—in that direction—that the golden path of the Mazeway glowed. It gleamed for his eyes alone; it neither glowed nor showed for others.

And now it led to the great quay of Lisbon, on this, the 1st day of November, in the year 1755.

And this, of course, was impossible.

More often than not Nate had not known where (or when) he had been, in his progress from outside to outside through the Maze. But he knew now. And he knew what would happen there at the great broad curving quay where the mobbing multitudes of Lisbon pressed and waited for the salvation which would never (in this world) come: that the sea, which had retreated at the first shock of the quake, would come rushing—flooding—roaring—crashing back. How those in front were unable to escape because of those who still pressed frantically forward, pressing in from behind. How, at last, sea and earth met together in one great and grinding blow, the quay and all who thronged upon it slipping, falling, sinking. . . . And the waters rolling, at first restlessly, then at length peaceably, rolling, rolling over all.

There was no way through. There was no way around.

It behooved him, then, to find a way back. And this could be only a way back for himself. To retreat through the Maze and face again the horror was not to be thought of. That he would ever again locate another way onward was, while perhaps not utterly impossible, unlikely in the most extreme degree. What then remained? To remain as an exile and a castaway in the eighteenth century? There were worse things. He had two functioning hands, a strong back, a good mind, a store of common sense, and a wealth of knowledge and experience beyond that of others of the time. He could make out, as his own age put it. Perhaps the Chulpex would come through and find him, perhaps not; perhaps not till after he was dead. All that remained (thus concluding the pulsating thought of a second) was to turn in his tracks and head for the broad, high places of the city, and safety.

He went onward toward the harbor, following the gleaming, glowing Mazeway. Dust from thousands of shattered buildings filled the air and cast a pall of darkness before the face of the astonished sun, and the Maze-path, as it left the street of Lisbon and led, though aslant, straight enough up into the air, gleaming like a great beam of light. Below, one single man cried out to see the other single man walk up into the air as though he did but tread a steep, steep path. But no one else paused to look. And Nate passed through the golden circle to the Center of the Maze.

CHAPTER TEN

In the upper room of the fortified ranch in the lower Ozarks where he prepared his radio lectures on Revitalized Americanism and Lower Taxes—and incidentally, very incidentally—raised prized Tunis ewes at a deductible loss, John Augustus Horn was dreaming dreams and working out plans.

A safe man had to be groomed to assume the office of Speaker of the House; this was essential. The great change-over, whereby the United States was to be restored to its proper status as a republic and confederation (such as it had been prior to the unfortunate Compromise of 1850, which John Augustus Horn, perhaps alone among contemporary students of politics, clearly recognized as the Mortal Wound: the base surrender of the Whigs, the useless efforts to truckle to Abolitionism)—this change was to be accomplished by *entirely constitutional means*! No man loved the constitution more than Horn; it had to be cleansed of its corrosive accretions, that was all. Yes . . . Major Flint—he had better be made a General, a General in the as-yet-to-be organized American Republican Armies: the Army of Texas, the Army of California, and so on, one for each sovereign State—Flint, with the aid of his right-thinking allies, the Chulpex, would first take over the Soviet Union and China, of course. Then the decadent British Empire, Africa . . . after that, well, the timetable would be worked out in good time. Yes.

Then, the President and Vice-President of the United States, presented, cold turkey, with the unassailable facts, would resign. Public pressure alone would require that. A sudden thought occurred to the spare, freckled, tight-mouthed old man. He frowned, then, almost instantly, smiled. Of course, of course. The Vice-President would have to resign first, otherwise he would become President himself immediately on the resignation of the President. Yes . . . Horn made a note. Well. So. Then, naturally, the Speaker of

132

the House automatically succeeded to the Presidency. A safe man, a *safe* man.

Horn began to jot down a list of names. A form showing the members of the Houses of Congress in order of the rightness of their voting records (in committees, as well as on the floor) was in the top right-hand drawer of his vast, tidy desk; but Horn knew it almost by heart.

However, the Representative with the best voting record was not necessarily for this purpose the best. The Honorable Hughes Boynton ("Hughie Boy") Searles had ambitions; this was not bad; this was good—for the Welfare State, in removing from the workingman the fear of his children's certainly starving to death unless he worked for what wages his employer chose to pay him, had destroyed the man's *ambition*— that is, generally speaking, it was good. But in this case it formed a slight but definite impediment. John Augustus Horn was not ready to employ his huge and hard-earned fortune ("Left school at age ten to peddle mule harnesses. By age thirteen, owned largest entirely locally owned harness business in Scatt Smith County. Sold it to buy his first block of oil leases. Drilled first well by hand with aid of one negro man, brought him to Jesus. Well dry.") and to take the risks involved in working with these foreign Chulpex in order to place the powers of the American Presidency in Hughie Boy Searles's hands. No. Searles was entitled to a place of importance on the as-yet-to-be-formed Presidency Advisory Council . . . but not to the office of First Magistrate itself.

The likeliest candidate for *that* post (via the Speakership) seemed to be . . . Horn's hand paused. Chulpex. Foreigners. He hoped that none of them expected under any circumstances to *settle* in the United States! Certainly, they were entitled to a reward for their assistance, but the reward would have to be found somewhere else. Mars, maybe. Or Venus. Or—at most, at the very most—a limited number might be allowed to undertake contract labor in, say, New Guinea. He hoped that Flint would make them understand this clearly. The work of restoring the Electoral college to its proper function, extending the criminal syndicalism statutes to ban all forms of labor organizing, revival and up-scaling of property qualifications for the elective franchise, outlawing of sugar refining and milk pasteurizing: all, all of these stern and meritorious projects were essential—but none so essential as rigid immigration controls. Although—the idea came to him like a flash of heat lightning—might not a freer entrance of them as contract laborers into *the United States* prove even more effective as a means of keeping the cost of labor down? Down where it *belonged?* Of course it would. Of course it would!

John Augustus Horn smiled happily and made more notes.

Major Flint had long ago (it seemed long, long ago) sent "Jackson" off to try and relay messages about the necessity of intercepting and stopping Nathaniel Gordon. He hoped that by now the word had gotten to that vast, low-density planet, swarming like a termite-hill as it circled slowly around the cooling star which was Sun Sarnis. In fact, it might be that the Chulpex had already located Gordon, and cut him off. In such a case the goddamn gooks might have killed him. "I hope not," he said, aloud.

Jack Pace looked up. His dark face had gone somewhat sallow under its stubble of fresh, black beard. The two men marched with measured caution through a vast park-land in which they had seen two gigantic and snow-white stags, and nothing else. The truth of the matter was, that Jack Pace was frightened, terribly, terribly frightened. So much so that he had almost ceased to think about automobiles and women. He tried recalling them now, in this perhaps the least strange of the many places they had passed through, which was nevertheless most horribly strange to him. For a brief moment the old familiar images took on form once more: Bentleys, Rollses, Hispano-Suizas, long red Jaguars and cream-colored Cadillacs; queens and princesses and movie stars and wives of presidents . . . he would have them all: he: Jack Pace: standing at the right hand of Major Flint when Major Flint became governor or emperor or whatever it was . . .

The images faded, faded quickly.

" 'Hope not' what?" he asked, his voice low. There, bulging out of Flint's pocket was that damned crazy thing which was supposed to show him the way in and the way out, the way forward and the way back. Every time the Major looked into it along with the goblin—for so Jack had thought of Chulpex as a boy before he had ever seen one; so he continued to think of them, and would do so as long as he lived—when the Major and the goblin looked into that crazy stone to find out where they were and where they were going, the Major had him look into it too. He'd point here and there and ask Jack if he noticed this or that thing about some line here or there. Jack said he did, because it did no good if he said he didn't— the Major would just talk some more and move the stone.

But what if anything happened to the Major?

Jack would shoot the goblin, he would have to shoot the goblin, of course. Otherwise the thing would maybe kill him, and even if it only *touched* him— So he'd have to kill it first. He'd killed plenty of them back there at the bottom of the mine-shaft in Flint's Forge. They'd be poking through and telling him about all the great cars and women they were going to get him, and this in fact had helped him a lot to think clearly about this for the first time, but nobody could trust a goblin and he had his job to do and so he shot them and he'd shoot this one, too. And then what? He'd be stuck forever—never in a million years be able to figure out that stone thing. His ammunition would run out. And then what? And then what?

"Why," said Major Flint, "I hope not, that no goo— no Chulpex have killed that traitorous bastard, Gordon."

Jack Pace felt almost indifferent about Gordon. True, it was because of him that they were off, way off in this world of dreams and of nightmares so far that they might never get back. But the cause was dim and past by now. The present and the future were cold and menacing. "Save having to do it ourselves," he mumbled. Gordon. Cars. Girls.

Softly, his teeth clicking, Flint said, "But I don't *want* to be saved having to do it ourselves. What? 'Our—' No, no, Jack. Don't dare try. He's *my* bird, you hear? All my life, waiting . . . family before me . . . hundred eighty-odd years . . . now at last . . . now at last . . ." His voice died away.

And the Na 14 said, "Should we not pause to take food?"

His thoughts snapped back, Flint said sourly, "Live off your fat a while. You seem to have enough of it. Always eating. You can wait a while. Oh, what the Hell. Here. Take a can of pemmican. We won't stop, though."

That was another problem. How to get *rid* of the Chulpex. Afterward. Nuclear weapons? Poison gas? Poison? He walked along, brooding.

The Na 14 ate swiftly, greedily. The consumption of much protein was the only certainty in his present existence; that—and the knowledge of what it was doing to him. Otherwise, all had been uncertainty since he regained consciousness in the cave in the Land of the Red Fish. The Na 14 had not counted on such swift pursuit as that which encountered him there. It was unfortunate. But at least the eggs had hatched and he had killed all the male fry. The strange Na who had found and attacked him (from another Sire's-get, his aura was unfamiliar)—where was he?

The vivipar which called itself Flint said that it knew. That chulpechoid said that in return for the assistance of the Na 14 in the use of the to-it-unfamiliar tracking device, it would do various things: Inform the Na 14 where the strange Na was. Refrain from killing the female fry in the cave. Provide the Na 14 with protein until the resolution of its, the chulpechoid vivipar's, quest. And then assist the Na 14 in gaining the mastery of Red Fish Land and its planet. This appeared to be a clever chulpechoid. Perhaps some use could be found for it subsequently; if not, then it and the others of its species must be dealt with alike.

The Na 14 licked up the last of the protein, let the container fall, and peered over at the tracking device which the intelligent creature was now examining. He pointed. "There," he said. "There. That one line. So."

"Indeed," said Enoch ben-Jared, stroking his beard. "I am a writer of some fame myself. Or so I am assured. They tell me that I have not only written copiously, but in a variety of languages rather astonishing. Welcome, my fellow." And to Nate's mind, no longer dazed but still remembering vividly that it had lately *been* dazed, came the clear knowledge that ancient Enoch ever young was not employing one of those requisite hypocrisies called courtesy. He meant: you *are* welcome. He meant: you *are* my fellow.

More, there was more here than merely having safely walked through fire to a place where his feet were cool. More than being genuinely welcomed, more than being greeted as an equal by those whom he had previously regarded as infinitely his superiors. There was so much more that he was only just beginning to grasp it. *But, he was beginning—!*

Looking at the calm, enlightened faces about him, Nate said, "I understand now . . . that you are not 'The Masters of the Maze,' as one speaks of 'the Master' of a vessel. . . ."

The old man dressed in archaic Chinese costume smiled gently. A bullock wandered up and placed its muzzle on his shoulder. He rested a hand upon it, light as a breath. "You understand. It is a way. We are those who have ascended this way, finding understanding as we did so. Finding, next, complete understanding here, where there is neither north nor south, nor east nor west, nor up nor down. There is neither past nor future, and even *present* is recognized as being illusory. Here, then—to use a term no doubt familiar to you—here there is no *maya*."

Recognition sparked in Nate's mind. "You are the one called 'Old Fellow'!"

Still smiling his gentle smile, "Yes, I am Lao-tze," the old man said.

". . . you are those who have *become* Masters by virtue of having passed through the Maze to its Center!" he, Nate, concluded. "The imperishable fabric," he murmured. And still understanding continued to well up inside of him, like a spring through parched-dry sand. "And I? And I—?"

"You, too," said Enoch (ancient Enoch ever young), "are now one of us. You are one of the Masters. One of the Masters of the Maze. Therefore, welcome, and again, welcome . . . my fellow."

"Welcome," said Benjamin Bathurst; "my fellow."

"Welcome, my fellow," said King Wen, looking up from the square of earth on which he had circumscribed a circle and in which he was lining out his hexagrams.

Appolonius of Tyanna and all the scores of others greeted him and with the same words bade him welcome. It was this sage who, when the ritual was completed, said to him, "What new thing has our new fellow to tell to us?"

"The Chulpex are trying to break through," Nate began.

With a smile, Appolonius said, "This is not new. Is there a Maze? Then the Chulpex are trying to break through it. *'Forever, forever, with useless endeavor, / Is Sisyphus rolling / His stone up the mountain . . .'* "

Nate told them that the situation was no longer the same. "It is ever no more the same," said King Wen, in his deep, rolling voice. "It displays the paradox concerning change and permanence. The only permanent thing is change itself. The only new thing about the Chulpex is the thing that is old about the Chulpex: they are an aberration and their world is an aberration and the arm of the Maze on which it lies is itself an aberration. The nature of aberrations is not to endure; therefore the superior man does not concern himself with them."

Nate looked at him in perplexity. He was sure that he could and would make them see the danger, but already the urgency of the matter seemed a bit faded in the air of infinite calm which permeated the Center.

"Before," he said, "they were alone. Now they have allies. Before, they came through or attempted to come through, one by one. Now they're coming through in swarms and myriads. Some new urgency seems to have possessed them. I don't know what."

"Movement," muttered King Wen, continuing to sketch the straight and broken lines of his hexagrams. "Movement to, movement fro. The endless concourse of the atoms. The waters run into the sea, they arise from the sea in clouds of vapor, the clouds discharge their waters upon the earth, and thence they run into the sea once again. This process cannot be interfered with. The houses of the righteous and the houses of the wicked alike are washed down by the floods, and in the sea the capsized vessel allows the enlightened and the unenlightened alike to drown. Nature does not interfere, and neither can we."

"But Darius Chauncey . . . he's one of the Watchers . . . he told me that the only thing for me to do was to get to the Center and tell the Masters. Who was it who set up the system of Watchers in the first place? Who saw to it that the first Watchers were shown how to use the ward-stones? Wasn't it you? You took action then, why can't you take it now?"

King Wen sketched the two broken and one unbroken lines of Rising Thunder before he replied. "It is permitted to build dams and dig canals to restrain and to channel off the floods," he said. "Also, to construct vessels to go upon the waters and the seas. But to prevent the rains themselves and to drain the seas themselves, who may do this?"

And the Old Fellow said, as though to his bull, "There is that which is *Tao* and that which is not *Tao*. It has been observed that, '*Tao*, though the means of all motion, is itself motionless.'"

Nate paused, then asked, "Are you trying to tell me that it is impossible for you to take action against the Chulpex because you cannot? Or because you will not? Because you are literally incapable? Or because you think it would be improper? Is your refusal based on physical, or on metaphysical, grounds?"

O tenal Tenal asked, "Is there a difference?" O tenal Tenal, he had wandered away from the cities of Mars when the air of that planet was as rich as blood, and the wisdom and the wickedness of its seven hundred cities was without parallel. "The thief cannot steal because he is afraid of the wounds which will accrue. The thinker cannot steal because he is afraid of the inner shame which will accrue. One reason may be said to be physical, one reason may be said to be metaphysical: but both achieve the same result: one cannot steal. So there is no difference."

"But—"

O tenal Tenal said, "Moreover . . ." And the others joined in in the discussion. Intellectually, it was fascinating. Otherwise, it was frustrating. He tried to draw them pictures, he spoke to them of War. Famine. Pestilence. Death. They spoke to him of the necessity of change, the disorder of which was no disorder, for it resulted in permanence. If there were no change, chaos would result, and all things dissolve into their components, and the components in turn into theirs.

"But the Chulpex—"

"Genghis Khan."

"A thousand times worse!"

"A thousand times zero is zero."

"But their victory would result in a major change in the nature of life in the universe."

"Precisely why no major effort may be made to avert it. I am afflicted by the harsh brightness of the sunlight, I am oppressed by the sullen darkness of the night. I perish of heatstroke, I die from stumbling into a pit. Such is the nature of things. It is better than that the sun should go out or that it should burn both by day and by night. Yet it is essential neither that I suffer heatstroke nor falling. In the time of sun, I may remain indoors; likewise, in time of night. Or, desiring to go out, who prevents or what prevents my carrying either sunshade or lamp? Further: if, despite sunshade and despite lamp, still I perish, then obviously it is part of the fabric of all component things that I should do so."

Nate passed his hand in front of his face, shook his head.

"This is difficult," he said, low-voiced. "I had thought that mastery meant victory. Now I see that mastery means understanding and acceptance, and that this is the true victory. But I'm not philosopher enough to be 'above the battle' . . . I don't want to be. I can't take that dispassionate view of things, and I don't want to. Evidently there's a part of me to which enlightenment is not enough, a big part of me; and when the rest of me says, calmly and serenely, *All flesh must die*, that's the part that won't lie down and contemplate its navel—the part that says, *Let this little kid live to be eighty and not let him die in war while he's still a little kid.*

"Maybe I'm too new at all this. These allegories about floods and sunshades. You mean, those who are invaded can resist and maybe win. Maybe. But if the Chulpex break through and capture all the Maze and all the times and places and the rest of it that are connected to the Maze, then, eventually, hard as it is, *what's to prevent their getting here to the Center of the Maze?*"

O tenal Tenal lifted his hands, thin as spiders' legs, to his thin, dry lips. "In theory, nothing."

"Then," said Nate, "what's to prevent their wiping all of you—or, I'd better say, maybe—all of *us*—what's to prevent their wiping us all out here?"

"They would not wish to."

"Not wish to. How do you know? I see none but humans here. Superior humans, glorified humans, clarified humans, enlightened humans—but: humans. And all our thoughts arise out of the structure of the human psyche. *But Chulpex are not human!* Is the structure of their psyche such that increased powers can benefit it? Suppose that instead of the cancer being cured, a super-cancer results? Will a superior wolf learn mercy, justice and humility if there is no pre-existing comprehension of such qualities? or perhaps even the ability to comprehend them? You, sir. King Wen? What do you think is the likelihood of any Chulpex gaining full enlightenment? Partial enlightenment? You, O tenal Tenal. Sir. Would you create a race of super-thieves? You tell me things like, The superior man is not active—thereby risking gross interference with essential nature and the eternal flux—but he is passive, and thereby permits things to arrange themselves in accordance with their innate necessities."

"True," said King Wen.

Nate asked, "What are the innate necessities of aberrant things?"

King Wen was silent.

"Isn't there a difference between the quality of Yang and Yin, which is coöperation, and the duality of Ahriman and Mazda, which is conflict?"

King Wen was silent.

There was a long, long silence, and then Appolonius of Tyana said, softly, "Cast the changes, my fellow, Wen. This is the process which you perfected, here in the Perfect Center, the Dragon Castle on the Floor of the Sea, the Yellow Castle at the Dark Pass between the Terrace of Light and the Purple Hall of the City of Jade, which same is the Space of Former Heaven. You sent it out to the Outer Worlds from here, the Germinal Vesicle at the Borderline of the Snow Mountains, the Primordial Pass between the Empire of Greatest Joy and the Lands Without Boundaries. In the Outer Worlds the changes may also be cast; how much more so here, the Altar upon which consciousness and life are made. My fellow, Wen, cast the changes."

King Wen was silent.

Lao-tze said, "Let darkness give birth to light. Let the unseen be seen, the unconscious become conscious. Wen, my fellow, cast the changes."

King Wen sighed. To Nate he said, "We are the Masters of the Maze, but we are within, the Maze is without. You had heard of microcosm and macrocosm; now you understand, also, the introcosm and the exocosm. Everything flows, everything flows. You did not only come to the Center, the Center also came to you. The past recedes, the future approaches; the future recedes, the past approaches. You alone stand in your place, unmoved, in the eternal present. Here, around me, are the sixty-four hexagrams of the broken and unbroken lines, the Yin and the Yang, the weak lines and the strong lines: all the possible permutations of all the possible possibles. Here in my hands are the broken and unbroken sticks of the fragrant and sacred yarrow. Put your thoughts in order and formulate your question."

Again there was silence. Then Nate said, " *'Shall the Masters of the Maze take such action as may be necessary to prevent the Chulpex from breaking through, overcoming the Outer Worlds, and penetrating the Center?'* "

King Wen cast the changes, throwing down the yarrow sticks again and again, until the pattern of the pre-eminent now lay clear for all to see, arranged in the six lines of the hexagram. He pondered it, considering. *"Progress,"* he said, at last. "Above, the trigram *li*: strong, weak, strong. Unbroken, broken, unbroken. Yang, Yin, Yang. The lower trigram: *'Receptive,'* Yin, Yin, Yin . . ."

Lao-tze said, "The one who is to bring about progress—that is you, Nathaniel Gordon—is dependent upon others—that is us, the other, older Masters. Nevertheless, we regard ourselves as your equal, and are willing to follow you. You have much *li*: clarity. Therefore you do not abuse your influence." He put his head a trifle to one side and made a slight humming noise. He pointed. "One moving line, as it is called, you see. *'An enlightened ruler and an obedient servant.'* King Wen and Nathaniel Gordon. Although we, including Wen, are willing to follow you by taking action, in this case you are called 'servant' because you are willing to follow Wen by submitting to the judgment of his oracle. *An enlightened ruler and an obedient servant; all are in accord; remorse vanishes.* Wen, what is your commentary?"

King Wen considered, briefly, before saying, "A man strives onward in association with others, whose backing encourages him. This dispels any cause for regret over the fact that he does not have enough independence to triumph unaided over every hostile turn of fate." He turned from considering the pattern of the yarrow sticks and said to Nate. "Is it clear? The pattern is by no means uniformly auspicious."

"That much is clear. Yes."

"This moving line, then, the top line of the lower trigram, *k'un*, is broken, and is near to *li*, clarity. It refers to associates; a common trust posseses them; the subject is trusted by all about him; therefore the auspices are mainly favorable. The rest you see for yourself."

Nate nodded. The auspices were favorable for the success of the project. They were not necessarily favorable for himself. He told them so, and they agreed. They asked him if he were nonetheless willing, and he agreed.

"Clearly, yours is the path of *Tao*," said Lao-tze. "The classics tell us that the Dragon wishes to devour the Sun and that the Phoenix dances before the Dragon. Is it in order to lead the Dragon away from the Sun? You must follow the path of *Tao*."

Many had sought to find what he had found, and had they indeed found it? Many had thought so. They had climbed mountains and gone into deserts, isolated themselves in forests and upon islands. They had sought God and they had sought Devil, Christ and Antichrist, immortality and annihilation, nirvana and revolution, in monastic cell and in prison cell alike, surrendering family, scanting food, denying former and familiar friends, refusing their bodies intimate and basic demands, doing deeds which in other contexts had been deemed wrong but in these were considered right. They had gone into exile, they had gone into the fire, faced death and courted death, defied death, and walked with death as with a familiar companion. Some had burned Jews in Spain, and then gone off, to be burned in turn, in Japan. Religion had inspired some, irreligion (that most demanding of all religions) had inspired others. There were those who had given themselves over to nationalism and those who had given themselves over to internationalism; still others had yielded to the insidious and shameless thing which, using the name of internationalism, is really the nationalism of another and foreign country. Inspired by impure motives and doing pure things, inspired by pure motives and doing impure things

. . . There was no end to it. No greed was comparable to the appeal of self-sacrifice.

And now it was the turn of Nathaniel Gordon.

He had barely had the taste of honey in his mouth, and now he was bound to depart again. The new-gained ability, the new-found knowledge, the enlightenment and calm, all, all, would depart from him with his leaving the Center—some abruptly, some gradually. He who had learned levitation must now walk again. For a while he had been almost one with and among the greatest. Now he was once more just Nate Gordon. Certain ironic aspects of this passed through his mind.

"Communist Chulpex Ate My Wife," he muttered.

"Farewell, my fellow."

"Farewell . . ."

Life is a dream and the dream is but a dream itself. All doth pass. All doth pass.

"Everything flows . . ."

The Center flowed away from him, he flowed away from the Center. Configurations and permutations perplexed and passed his eyes. He did not leave as he had entered and the scenes he saw were new and strange to him, but yet familiar in that they were unfamiliar and old by virtue of their continual newness. He was obliged to tarry awhile among the nonhuman but kindly Theriowol whilst, with tears of grief and great cries of helpless anguish, they burnt to the ground the city in which they dwelt as the bicentennial and blazing horde of meteors passing overhead informed them that the time for this had come; then they turned and toiled off into the wilderness to seek another site. Six days he dwelt amongst the Lost Tribes by the shores of the Sambatyon until, on the seventh, the river ceased to flow, and he walked across its bed in the Sabbath calm and quiet. He was caught up a while in a procession of dancing, jerking, twitching, moaning sufferers en route to seek relief at the great shrine of St. Vitus; some said that their sufferings were caused by demons, some, that the bite of a spider had caused it; others muttered that it was a poison created by the rust upon the rye which made their bread: all, however, attributed Nate's odd manner and speech and his haste in getting on, to the madness—whatever its cause—and so, kindly but firmly, helpful participants in the pilgrimage seized his arms and danced him along, *two and one, one and two, St. Vitus, pray for us, St. Vitus, intercede for us, one and two and two and one . . .*

He came to the caves of ice at last and in time, not pausing to look closely at the things frozen there, but wondering if he were perhaps destined to be frozen there himself; but at last he managed to open a hatchway in a huge door on the lowest slope of the lowermost cave. It was by no means *warm* in there, but it was perceptibly less cold. It smelt worse, though. Much worse. And it continued to go on smelling worse—rank and dank and acrid and clammy and . . . and something else, something which had been briefly familiar to him. He descended level after level, like someone in a bad dream or in a (bad, *ex officio*) novel or story by Merrit or Lovecraft. The latter, at least, he recalled, had been obsessed with unpleasant odors. *And* with cold. The former had merely cultivated a large, country garden consisting entirely of poisonous plants. And Lovecraft had also been obsessed with the theme of humans lending themselves or selling themselves to the service of alien creatures. Like Major Flint. In fact, Nate reflected, Lovecraft might have gotten along quite well with Major Flint. Their social views had much in common.

It was a superior war-Na who recognized Nate immediately from having seen him fleeing across the velvet plain where the great scarlet birds were tended by the dwarfs. He hesitated. The 'Murriste-Sire should be informed at once, of course. On the other hand, it would be great, high-nest identity-assertion were he himself to bring this creature before the 'Murriste-Sire. It had been bad, quite bad, returning and having to tell the Sire that, though the pursuing war-Nas had indeed found the Gate through which the sought-for alien had vanished once again into the Many-Pathed Way, they had been unable to find his trail again after that. Great was the Sire's wrath, and, indeed, the superior war-Na had at that time expected nothing more than that his Sire would then and there claim an occasion for justifiable anger-outlet.

He seized a work-Na who was, like at least half of those present, pointing and waving his arms and chattering astonishment—the other half were running busily about, often in opposite directions, doing nothing—and said to him, "Convey word to the Sire that the war-Na 102 'Murriste 634 has found the chulpechoid that escaped us before. At once, the work-Na!"

"At once, thus, the war-Na!"

If this message were to be, and in view of this confusion it might well be, the first intelligence of the matter to reach the Sire, this would be good for the war-Na. It could not in any case, be bad for him. Unless—and he stood stock-still and almost shrilled his sudden fear—unless the message reached the Sire and the chulpechoid vanished again! In such a case the war-Na might regard himself fortunate if he were merely directed to cease to take food.

What the correct manner of approaching the chulpechoid at the present place and under the present circumstances might be, the superior war-Na did not know. The instructions at the previous occasion had been, very simply, "Capture and return." But there were none but war-Nas there, highly disciplined. This was an encounter at a crossing-level of the upper ramps, all sorts and classes were present, there was no unity. To pause and search out war-Nas, to convince of the correctness of yielding to his, the war-Na 102's, orders— this meant time, time, precious time.

Thinking, acting quickly, the war-Na 102 approached the chulpechoid according to the ancient and prescribed rule of peacefully approaching the war-Na of another Sire-swarm: all four arms held away from the body, palms down. He did not, of course, know the vivipar's language; fortunately he had been spared training in the disgusting ways of the vivipar. The concept of bearing one's young alive was revolting in the extreme. A war-Na, however, is trained to repress his own natural emotions. Arms out, palms down, 102 'Murriste 634 approached the chulpechoid, neither slowly nor hastily.

It was true: the creature was intelligent. It had been walking rather aimlessly, but on perceiving the approach of the superior war-Na, it halted. The object in its hands (deformed, stunted life-form, having only two), it slowly placed between its legs to secure it; then it, too, held its arms out, palms down.

"This is well, the vivipar," the war-Na observed.

"Take me to your— ah, the Hell with that," said Nate. "We'll just play it cool, as befits the ex-Superior Man."

"Proceed ahead of me, the vivipar. Thus, as I indicate with my upper hands, thus. Do you not understand—the object? It appears to indicate no danger. You may take it up as before. Thus, thus."

Arristemurriste received the message impassively. That the chulpechoid vivipar had appeared where he had, indicating that an entrance to and exit from the Many-Pathed Way lay above, was a matter to be stored up for future consideration. Either the knowledge of this Gate had been forgotten as the race moved in toward the cooling center of the planet, or else it had opened up subsequently. What the purpose of the creature was in coming here, Arristemurriste could not know. He was the second, but the first, occupying the designation . . . the Sire could not be bothered with recalling the syllables of gibberish . . . this first creature had said that the other was dangerous and treacherous. It might be so. It might be that the converse was so. Arristemurriste reserved judgment; meanwhile he had sent for the Na 32 'Gorretta 502. The latter was assisted into his presence.

"Ordinarily," the 'Murriste-Sire reminded him, "Nas which return without having fulfilled their directives are assumed to be in possession of defective qualities which would result in their future failure as well. Therefore they have always been directed to cease to take food."

"Thus, the Sire."

"But in your case it has seemed that the fault lay rather with that aberrant body, the Na 14 'Parranto 600. Therefore the Sires are in agreement that you should for the present continue to live. Furthermore, you have been instructed in one of the vivpar languages. You were in contact with the second vivipar, who has unaccountably appeared among us. What is your impression concerning it?"

"The Na recalls that this creature seemed somewhat amenable to reason. The Na was of course unspeakably shocked when this creature attempted to destroy the fry that the Na 14 had taken away in eggs—but on further reflection it has seemed to the Na that, knowing about the Chulpex, this creature associated the fry only with the Na 14, and on hearing that the Na 14 attempted to take my life—"

"Thus. So. The Sire follows your train of reasoning. It may be. Here comes the vivipar now. It will require your services as translator for us to understand it. Direct it to speak concerning its relationship with the other."

It came as merely another shock to Nate, and by no means the biggest (not after seeing even what could only have been the tiniest of glimpses of the swarming, swarming Chulpex-life), to hear the translucent, six-limbed thing supported between two other translucent six-armed things speak to him in the suddenly well-remembered voice of "Jackson."

"Previously," he said, cautiously replying to the question, "I was hostile to Major Flint. But I am so no longer. My reason," he anticipated the next question, "is that I realize that the victory of the Chulpex is certain and Major Flint has promised me a position of power in return for my aid."

Arristemurriste pondered. The answer was so logical as to

require no further interrogation. But the answer conveyed another question inside of it, and this the Sire proceeded at once to ask. "What form is this aid of yours to take?"

Nate looked up at the huge figure, and despite himself swallowed hard. Then he said, "I am to show the Chulpex a route whereby they may circumvent all obstructions and enter into swift conquest of all."

CHAPTER ELEVEN

Major Flint decided, abruptly, unalterably, that he had had enough of chasing Nate Gordon through the nine Earths, the nine Heavens, and the nine Hells. "Let's get back where we belong and get to work," he said to Jack Pace.

Who was so relieved that it felt like waves of cold water were flowing down his legs. *Back where they belonged!* Away forever from weird walls and weird halls, weird worlds and weird things! Home! To clean their weapons and organize their forces, drill their troops. Of course the regular army and navy was bound to come over to their side as soon as the issue was made clear; Major Flint had said that all along. Jack's eyes flickered as he thought of the quick, clean job of putting down the mobs which would follow. And then—and then, boy! Time to cut the turkey and pass out the pie!

Cars. Women. Girls. Cars. *God!*

Get started right away. Head back home. Now.

Only—

"What about the bug?" he asked, in a casual tone of voice, not moving his eyes.

"Too useful to lose. It's not in it with the other bugs. Don't know exactly what its game is or if it's got much of a following, but—sound old principle: Divide and rule. We'll see. We'll see."

The bug itself was digesting the last of the venison. Exercises had given them all an appetite, particularly, it seemed, the Na 14. Rather than part with more of the canned pemmican, Major Flint had told Jack to shoot the next buck they saw. It was white, as they were all, in this place, wherever it was; and showed no fear. It was easy as jacklighting. The bug hadn't shown any interest in the weapon, though you might have thought it would. All it seemed to be thinking about was food; it had lapped up the blood, even. Made Jack sick to his stomach to think of it now. So there it was, like a python gorged with a goat, making slobby noises. They had to wait until it was ready, or able, to get onto its feet again before they could move on. Major Flint explained that they were going back. It didn't say anything.

It may have been something in the sunlight of the next place they were passing through. It reminded Jack of the effect of the ultra-voilet lamp he'd seen once or twice in the new barbershop someone had opened down in Groatsville—before the novelty wore off and everyone went back to patronizing the old barbershop with the permanent card game in the dirty back room. Or, again, it may have had nothing to do with it. Jack hadn't had much time to think about it.

The three of them were just coming out from a grove of trees which were altogether the wrong color and which cast shadows that made him uneasy, when Jack heard Major Flint give a cry of such short, startled horror as to be almost a squawk. He whirled around and he screamed.

The goblin seemed to have doubled in size. Its chitinous exterior was cracked and riven and a serous matter oozed from the rifts. It made little noises of pain. Then it said something about "Protein" and something about "Sire." Or it might have been, "Desire." Then, with a sudden, swift movement, it swooped down on Major Flint and seized him up with its four arms and bit into him and bit out of him and began to eat.

Jack Pace shot it and shot it again and shot it again and again. It fell down, not far from where Flint lay, flopping and bleeding and making noises that no one could listen to. Jack never stopped screaming, not even after he threw down his carbine and ran and ran and stumbled and fell and got up and ran again.

Major Flint and the Na 14 lay under the unnatural light of the sun that was so alien to both of them, and they watched each other die.

Nate's proposal was so close to an absolute congruity with Arristemurriste's needs and desires that it would have required the most difficult of efforts not to agree with it. True, the other Sires had conceded that the breakthrough program must be accelerated. True, the breakthrough program had

been accelerated. But the program had gone on at much the
same pace for so long a period that neither the psychology
nor the facilities of the Chulpex were capable of a very great
increase. Such an increase as was accomplished was capable
of somewhat of a considerable spur when Flint first appeared. And the fact that a detachment of war-Nas had been
sent in search of Nate Gordon now fit in quite well, curiously enough, with Nate Gordon's plan as described to the
'Murriste-Sire.

"A mass breakthrough is the only answer."

Thus! If a mere few hundreds of thousands could safely go
in search of Nate Gordon and safely return (even if without
him)—if it were possible for them to pass despite those who
watch and those who fight—then it followed surely that an
unlimited number had nothing to fear in the way of failure.

"All the Chulpex must advance, without exception."

Thus! Rigid, diligent, slow to imagine, loath to change, the
Chulpex found great difficulty (which, for the most part, they
did not even recognize as difficulty) in affecting a change of a
few degrees in any area involving individual effort. Told,
however, to arise or to descend, to advance or to retreat, they
responded instantly . . . automatically . . . so mindlessly,
in fact, as to make the term *willingly* almost inapplicable.

*"In this way they will overcome not only opposition but
the possibility of opposition by their sheer weight of numbers."*

Thus! Doubtless the vivipar, through inherent inferiority of
mind, thinking mainly of what he expected would be his own
interests, overlooked the almost certain likelihood that there
must of necessity be a measure of opposition. No matter.
Assuredly, numbers of Chulpex would be killed. Again, no
matter. What mattered was not that this Na or that Ma
should live one cycle more or one cycle less. What mattered
was the assurance of life-through-life: the continued existence of the Chulpex race. Indeed, even if—theoretically, of
course—any considerable portion of the Chulpex swarms
should lose their lives in attaining a victorious breakthrough,
even this was of no major or long-term significance. But let
the Many-Pathed Way come altogether within their grasp,
and the Chulpex would repopulate until their former (that is,
their present) numbers were restored. And more! And more!
And more!

No more crawling further and further into this burrow of
a dying planet in search of warmth! An end to stagnation,
once and for all! The shameful memories of such aberrations

as Arrantoparranto, who had refused to breed and who had wanted a percentage of the egg-clusters destroyed, and of the Na 14 (*Parranto* 600!) who had vilely stolen eggs in the hopes of becoming an independent Sire!

"It is well, the vivipar," declared Arristemurriste. "Whither do you intend to lead us?"

"First to our own world. From there a multitude of Gates and arms of the Maze extend."

Two thoughts occurred to the 'Murriste-Sire, so closely together that he could not tell which had come first. He pushed his massy bulk up from his dais and glared. His Nas trembled. Nate took a half-step backward. "Let there be no tricks!" warned Arristemurriste. "Do not think to lead us into a trap! You will go, not first, not last, from either position you might think to escape; the midst would not do if you are to give directions . . . So. Thus. You will go in the second phalanx. From there it will be easy to send directions to the front, but therefrom you cannot escape. Does the vivipar understand?"

"It is understood."

The great body settled down a trifle. The great mouth posed the second question. "What is the width of the path or arm along which we are to travel? This information is necessary in order to calculate how long it will take the entire Chulpex race to make the traversal."

Nate reminded him that ordinary considerations of dimensional mensuration did not apply, including the temporal. "But one thing should be mentioned. The Maze, too, has its systole and its diastole, though this process does not occur with any resembling frequency in metabolic time. Nor is it uniform on all arms. In fact, little may be said about it, other than that it does occur—and that it is about to occur on the arm which we will make use of for the traversal. During the period of diastole this arm will thus be much 'wider' and this of course will enable the traversal to be accomplished in an incomparably shorter period of metabolic time."

"Enough, the vivipar, for now. You may take food, but do not leave this chamber even to rest. The Sire will have you informed at the time he next requires you. Go—"

The decision was made. The word was given, the other Sires informed, the plans coördinated. They might have been condensed into three words.

Up!
Out!
All!

There were intended to be no exceptions and therefore, of course, there were none. Even those who had been directed to cease to take food and those penned in the anger-pits were not excepted. Possibly in the Warmer Worlds new directives might be issued concerning them; perhaps not. It made no difference. They were Chulpex. All Chulpex were to go.

All.

Those weak from not taking food were to be assisted. Hatchlings old enough to grasp securely were to ride upon the shoulders of the Mas, those too young would be held in the hands of other Mas. Some concern had to be entertained lest prolonged exposure to adult body temperature might effect adversely the unhatched eggs, which also were to be carried in the Mas' hands. But this could not be avoided. A percentage of loss had to be expected. Again, under these circumstances—but only under these—the loss had to be considered as being balanced by the gain.

Should not a rear guard be left behind?

No, decided the Sires.

Were the very generators to be abandoned and unmanned?

Yes, decided the Sires.

It was to be understood that this world, the dying satellite of Sarnis, the dying sun, was finished forever. Let no one think, for any reason, to creep back to the familiar nests and cells and swarm-houses, to flee or sneak back to spurious safety. The entire race would leave, en masse, and leave forever, its ancestral world, to find in the Warmer Worlds which now lay ignorantly awaiting them a richer life, vaster than ambition could imagine. Millions becoming billions, and billions becoming thousands of billions. Undreamed of warmth, unheard of protein, solids enough for all—

Up from the lowest nests, out from the cells and the swarm-houses moved the hordes. Without hesitation, without fear, without pause or panic, the exodus began. It flowed like some unprecedented river through the vast opacity which was the gate. True, the sight of this river as it twisted and turned and coiled and angled and looped in its flow down the arm of the Maze, this sight brought cries of astonishment. But not of alarm. No Chulpex was or could ever be afraid of something that every other Chulpex was doing. The gray-white tide flowed and rippled and surged; those in the center could barely see the sides; soon, soon enough, those entering could no longer see those who had entered first, so great was the distance.

As for those who had entered first, they never looked behind.

Nate Gordon was placed so that Arristemurriste could see him, and so that his directions could be quickly conveyed to the front. But no directions ever came. For long the great 'Gorretta-Sire was so bemused by what was happening that he neither spoke nor desired to. But by and by a wonder began to arise in him. Presently he did speak. "Let word be conveyed to Arristemurriste that Arrettagorretta desires to know in advance of our exit, in order that he may alert his war-Nas." This was but reasonable. Reasonable, too, was the placing of most of the war-Nas in advance of the work-Nas, with the Mas and the hatchlings, fry and eggs next; with the rest of the war-Nas bringing up the rear.

Multicycle after multicycle, the war-Nas had drilled and trained. Now at last they were going to have the chance to act, to fight, to conquer, and to slay.

The 'Murriste-Sire considered the question of the 'Gorretta-Sire. He, too, had been long lost in his own thoughts. Now he blinked and he reflected. It was warm and it was stuffy, but that was to be expected. "Attend, the vivipar," he said.

Nate swerved and turned his head. His face was pale. The stench and sound were overpowering. Arristemurriste looked at it and then Arristemurriste could no longer see it. "What is this?" he cried, disturbed. "The vivipar! The chulpechoid! Where is it?" But it was not to be found.

"It may have fallen, it may be trampled, it is necessary to us! Take care—take care—see that the vivipar is not trampled!"

But the vivipar was not to be found. Alarm gave way to suspicion, suspicion to a growing conviction of un-rightness. "Halt! Halt!" cried Arristemurriste. "*Halt!*"

His chief aide-Na said to him, "We cannot halt now, the Sire. It is that the pressure of those multitudes behind us prevents us."

"Then send word behind us, even to the very last ones, that all are to halt—and if there are any who have not yet entered, they are *not* to enter! All this must stop—the vivipar must be found—I desire that the situation be re-examined— send word, the aide-Na! Send word!"

Word was long, long in going; reply was long, long in returning. And all the while the great procession rolled on, flowed on, pressed on. Voices were heard, too, remarking on the heat. Disturbed at the heat. Suffering from the heat—

"The Sire, the Sire!"

"Speak! Speak!"

"All have entered, the Sire. All! But none can halt. The aide-Na does not understand, the aide-Na is confused, none can halt, none halt, the aide-Na is confused—"

Arristemurriste looked up sharply. A new blast of heat struck at him with a new intensity. The golden glow ahead was obscured by a dull red curtain which he had never seen before. Never seen before, but he knew—suddenly!—he knew. He knew, and he roared and bellowed and dug in his limbs, neither noticing nor caring how many were crushed beneath and by him. Slowly, slowly, with infinite toil and infinite pain, the 'Murriste-Sire turned. And all around and under and below him the vast swarm swept inexorably onward and apace.

John Joseph Horn stared and blinked and stared again. A mere moment ago he had been on his way to pay a brief visit to his prize Poland China boar-pigs—the name had been making him doubly uneasy for years now, for all that it was old and pre-political; still, there might be room for a change: All-Americans? Texarkansas? Liberty Swine? hmmm, mmmm— and then like a burst of fireworks on a summer sky, the Maze flashed and whirled and sparkled and after that, seemingly, nothing, and a hell of a lot of it: and now this.

This was an unpaven city street where pigs (definitely not prize Poland China) rooted in the loose garbage and the freely scattered refuse of chamber pots. A dairyman milked a filthy cow into a filthy pot. The numerous grocery stores were all half saloons, swimming with spittle, swarming with flies and coarsely, brutally drunken men and women and children. An emaciated and malarial-looking family of emigrants squatted in their battered wagon drawn by slat-thin hoses whose harness sores stank abominably.

Horn stared, beginning to tremble, and aghast. He felt old. He felt sick. He felt terrified, foreboding and alone. A consumptive newsboy coughed in his face, flapped his wares. "Paper, Cap'? Magnetic telegraft report from Washin'on City, Cap'. 'Nauguration of General Pierce ... 'S matter, Cap'? Got the epizootic?"

It must not be thought that Horn did not understand. He understood perfectly well. He had wanted to bring back the past. And the past had brought him back, instead.

"I never expected it," Nate said. "I never thought of this happening to me."

"But you understand why, now, surely?"

Slowly, slowly, he said that he did. "It's because I was willing to make the sacrifice?—that's why I didn't have to?"

That was why. "By allowing things to occur, you allowed them to occur to you; by allowing them to happen, you allowed them to happen to you; by permitting instead of committing, by submitting to be passive instead of insisting upon being active, you have escaped the necessity of becoming the object of action," said King Wen.

And Enoch (ancient Enoch ever young) said, with a mild smile: "More simply: you gave, therefore you received."

And he said, "Welcome, my fellow."

It may be doubted that any of the Chulpex realized that it was into their own sun that they were led. Dying, that sun was, but it was not yet dead. Much of its substance had, over the course of eons, been consumed; but much of it was still left. Inexorably, mindlessly, Sun Sarnis exerted its gravitational pull and gathered relentlessly to its burning bosom the children who had sought to leave it. Here and there one or two or a few of them were swept and eddied into a nook or niche and for a while escaped. But then came the dancing, darting minotaurs, who killed them all; then vanished.

It may have been a triggering action, it may have been simply because the time for it had come. Sun Sarnis exploded outward in a burst of light which there were no eyes to see and a burst of noise which there were no ears to hear. It licked up the dust and the debris of the void, it devoured its planets one by blazing one, till nothing was left of the world of the Chulpex: hives, cells, swarms, and echoing, burning chambers. Then it fell in upon itself.

Distant astronomers observed, noted, described, announced. Eventually it was all quite forgotten.

Arristemurriste had forgotten even that that was his name. Only two things survived in the mind trapped behind the charred brain-case. One was its own, its terrible, terrible pain. The other was the recollection that somewhere, somewhere, existed the cave wherein the fry hatched of the Na 14's stolen eggs were lodged. And the 'Murriste-Sire could not die until it had seen the Mas among the fry grow to an age to mate. Until then, until he had assured the continued existence of the Chulpex race, the release of death was and must be denied.

Darius Chauncey saw the great and grieviously injured creature come crawling out on three limbs. He knew what he

had to do, but in order to do it he had to pass it. It clawed
out and lunged at him, but he dodged beneath its head. The
derringer concealed beneath the floor of his bedchamber had
only two great, green cartridges in it, and he fired both of
them into the Chulpex-Sire's head. He yoked a hundred oxen
and dragged it by night and by torchlight to the shore of the
sea, where one of his ships made it fast with ropes and took
it out of sight of land. Dolphins butted at it and fish tore at
it. And when, after two days, it had not moved, they cut the
ropes. It floated ashore, eventually, or what was left of it did.
The lions and the jackals worried it and the sun and the stars
and the curious moon shone down upon it, but presently it
was no more.

"I don't know yet," Nate said. "Of course, I will see that
the Watchers are informed. They don't have to guard against
Chulpex any more. But . . . something still has to be done,
or not done, or . . . For as long as the Maze exists, its
Gateways will be entered. Unless it is possible to seal it. We
must consider this. As for myself, well—
"Even if I don't stay on here, and I think that, probably, I
won't, but even so: I'm not as I was and will never be again.
My past ambitions were absurd, comparatively. I have a
thousand thousand Europes . . . and Asias . . . and Afri-
cas, Americas . . . to visit. If they are still there. If having
done all this hasn't, somehow, changed and upset everything."
Lao-tze arose and walked over to his bull. He turned from
the beast's side, back to look at Nate. "Time," he said, "is in
the mind. You suppose that changing an event in the past
will change an event in the present or future, but this is not
so, as you will see. For have we not shown you that, despite
our use of the words, there is no present, past, or future?
There is only an eternal *now*. That is the secret of the
Maze. One event cannot, therefore, cause another. Each
event is coexistent with all the others. In the 64 hexagrams
of the *Yi* we have an arbitrary representation of all the
infinite possible presents, each independent of all the others.
We can move from one 'now' to another along the straight
line of clock time, or we can cross from one event to another
by other routes, such as the Maze. It is all there, and from
here, at the center of time, we can reach any part of it,
simply by turning our attention to it. We exist in one event
by forgetting the rest."
He mounted the bull. "The Maze, you see," he said, "is

only our most well-worn path." He smiled, and slowly rode away.

The tribe lived in the early middle of the Dreaming Times, although they did not know that their descendants would call it that. The arrival of the stranger caused some surprise, some wonder as well. Not that he was white, this was not the wonder. The color of living men, obviously, was black. White was the color of ghosts. The wonder was as to *whose* ghost he was: obviously, of some member of their tribe, or else he would not have appeared among them. It was a subject rich in occasion for talk. Eventually, an elderly but spry woman named Born when the Moon Fell Down, decided that he was the ghost of her father. He, too, in his later years, had been possessed of devils and had gibbered and shrieked in this same way.

The matter, once settled, lost much of its interest. From time to time there was a bit of a hubbub when the ghost seemed to become momentarily sensible, for at such times he would lunge for one or another of the young women: then the Old Man would hit him smartly with his boomerang—not the big kangaroo-killing boomerang, for he was rather a kindly Old Man—the smaller one used for emu. None of the young women were of the proper degree of cousinship for The Ghost of the father of Born When The Moon Fell Down. Perhaps in thirty or forty years some might be born. Meanwhile, there were quite enough babies.

Otherwise the ghost gave little trouble. Sometimes he tried to wander away and had to be tugged along firmly by his daughter, who shared her share of the lizards and the snakes and the witchetty grubs with him—and even, occasionally, a piece of kangaroo or emu. He ate greedily and abstractedly. Sometimes he moaned and sometimes he screamed and sometimes he smiled and babbled contentedly about cars as he stumbled across the achingly empty continent which had never seen a wheel.

www.ingramcontent.com/pod-product-compliance
Lightning Source LLC
Chambersburg PA
CBHW022155260626
47155CB00018B/2055